THIS IS THE END OF THIS GRAPHIC NOVEL!

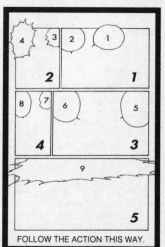

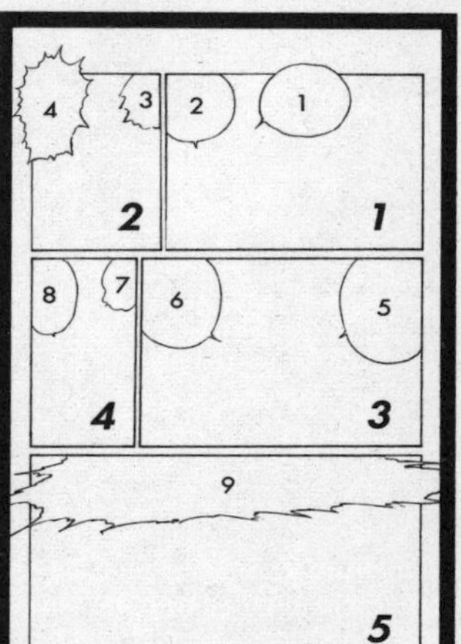

To properly enjoy this graphic novel, please turn it around and begin reading from right to left.

AUTHOR BIO

In addition to Asia and North America, the *YO-KAI WATCH* manga is now available in Europe as well! If you travel somewhere and see it, please pick one up for me as a souvenir!
—Noriyuki Konishi

Noriyuki Konishi hails from Shimabara City in Nagasaki Prefecture, Japan. He debuted with the one-shot *E-CUFF* in *Monthly Shonen Jump Original* in 1997. He is known for writing manga adaptations of *AM Driver* and *Mushiking: King of the Beetles*, along with *Saiyuki Hiro Go-Kū Den!*, *Chōhenshin Gag Gaiden!! Card Warrior Kamen Riders*, *Go-Go-Go Saiyuki: Shin Gokūden* and more. Konishi was the recipient of the 38th Kodansha manga award in 2014 and the 60th Shogakukan manga award in 2015.

STORY AND ART BY

NORIYUKI KONISHI

ORIGINAL CONCEPT AND SUPERVISED BY LEVEL-5 INC.

YO-KAI WATCH™

Volume 11

THE WAY OF THE SAMURAI

VIZ Media Edition

Story and Art by Noriyuki Konishi
Original Concept and Supervised by LEVEL-5 Inc.

Translation/Tetsuichiro Miyaki
English Adaptation/Aubrey Sitterson
Lettering/John Hunt
Design/Shawn Carrico

Printed in the U.S.A.

Published by VIZ Media, LLC
P.O. Box 77010
San Francisco, CA 94107

10 9 8 7 6 5 4 3 2 1
First printing, May 2019

STORY AND ART BY

NORIYUKI KONISHI

ORIGINAL CONCEPT AND SUPERVISED BY LEVEL-5 INC.

CHARACTER INTRODUCTION

NATHAN ADAMS

AN ORDINARY ELEMENTARY SCHOOL STUDENT. WHISPER GAVE HIM THE YO-KAI WATCH, AND THEY HAVE SINCE BECOME FRIENDS.

WHISPER

A YO-KAI BUTLER FREED BY NATE, WHISPER HELPS HIM BY USING HIS EXTENSIVE KNOWLEDGE OF OTHER YO-KAI.

JIBANYAN

A CAT WHO BECAME A YO-KAI WHEN HE PASSED AWAY. HE IS FRIENDLY, CAREFREE AND THE FIRST YO-KAI THAT NATE BEFRIENDED.

BARNABY BERNSTEIN
NATE'S CLASSMATE.
NICKNAME: BEAR.
CAN BE MISCHIEVOUS.

EDWARD ARCHER
NATE'S CLASSMATE.
NICKNAME: EDDIE. HE ALWAYS WEARS HEADPHONES.

USAPYON
A RABBIT-ESQUE YO-KAI IN A SPACESUIT.

HAILEY ANNE THOMAS
A FIFTH GRADER WHO IS A SELF-PROCLAIMED SUPERFAN OF ALIENS AND SAILOR CUTIES.

TOMNYAN
A CRYPTIC YO-KAI. WHAT ARE HIS REASONS FOR COMING TO THIS PART OF TOWN?

TABLE OF CONTENTS

CHAPTER 99:
DON'T FORGET THE BRAKES!
FEATURING SPACE LOVER YO-KAI USAPYON
ONCE AGAIN...I COULDN'T BEAT...THE TRUCK...
NNNNG!...
VRROOM
MNNGH...
MEOW...
VOOOOO VOOO OOOSH
MEOW?!
MEOOOOOW?!

KRA-K

WHAAAAAAAT?!

THUNGKT

LONG TIME NO SEE, JIBANYAN! ♪
TUMP TUMP TUMP...
TWITCH TWITCH
SPACE LOVER YO-KAI USAPYON
TA-DAH
I WAS FLYING MY ROCKET AND DECIDED TO STOP IN AND PAY YOU A VISIT! ♪
BAAM
I WISH... YOU HADN'T ...
TO FIND OUT MORE ABOUT THE ROCK-ET...
...CHECK OUT VOLUME 8 AND VOLUME 9! ♪
WILL YOU WAKE UP ALREADY ?!
I'M NOT ASLEEP!
HUFF HUFF
YOU OWE ME A BIG-TIME APOL-OGY!
YOU SAW ME! WHY DIDN'T YOU USE YOUR BRAKES?!
HUFF HUFF
TUMP TUMP
TO KEEP THE ROCKET LIGHT I DIDN'T ADD ANY BRAKES! THE ONLY WAY TO STOP IT...

...IS TO CRASH INTO SOMETHING. ♪
IT'S THAT SIMPLE!
YOU'VE DESCRIBED A MISSILE!
YOU KNOW... ♪ IT'S BEEN A WHILE SINCE I MADE A NEW FRIEND! I'M REALLY EXCITED! ♪
LET'S HANG OUT! ♪
YOU SHOULDN'T USE A FRIEND AS A LANDING PAD!
LET'S GO FOR A RIDE ON MY ROCK—
NEVER!
I'M NOT GOING TO RIDE A ROCKET THAT CAN'T EVEN STOP!
IT'LL STOP ONCE WE CRASH INTO SOMETHING!
WERE YOU EVEN PAYING ATTENTION?!
STOP BEING SO INCONSIDERATE! WHAT IF IT HITS A HUMAN BEING?!
DON'T WORRY! IF WE'RE IN DANGER OF HITTING A REAL LIVE PERSON...
RRMBLL...

I'LL USE THE **SELF-DESTRUCT SYSTEM** TO BLOW US INTO SMITHER-EENS! ♪
WE WON'T HURT ANY-ONE! ♪
IF YOU HAVE SPACE FOR ALL THAT... WHY NOT BRAKES?!
AND EXPLOSIONS ARE STILL DANGEROUS!
...
WHAAAAA
HE'S RIGHT!
I made a mistake!
VWEE
ANY-WAY ...
?
CLOMP
MEOW?!
SHUNK...
IT'S MY AUTO-MATIC BOARD-ING SYSTEM!
VWEEE
WHAT'S WITH ALL THESE GIZMOS?! ADD BRAKES!
ALL RIGHT THEN ...

ZWOOSH
LET'S GO! ♪
M-M-MEEE-OOW ...!
MMNGH MMNGH
GWOOO
HEEEEEEEELP MEEEEEEEE!
AGGGGGGH!
HEY!
FWOOOSH
WHERE ARE YOU GOING?!
I CAN'T HELP IT! I FELL OFF!
HEEEEEEEEELP!
AGGGH...
FOR CRYING OUT LOUD! HOLD ON!

FWOOSH
GRAB MY HAND!
!!!
AHHHH!
AHHHHH! I'M GOING TO CRASH!
SHWOOSH
WHOA! THAT WAS CLOSE!
!?/
VWOOOSH
KLIKT KLIKT
I'M SAFE!
WAIT... THERE ARE NO BRAKES! WE'RE GOING TO CRASH!
JUST LEAVE IT TO ME!

KA-DOOOM
URRRNGH
TWITCH
TWITCH
YOU REALLY... SHOULD...
TWITCH
TWITCH
I'LL ADD BRAKES...
PSSSSH...

CHAPTER 100:
A NEW YO-KAI APPEARS!!
FEATURING CRYPTIC YO-KAI TOMNYAN

I'M HOME.

UGGGN...
HICCUP
MMNGH
MMNGH

!!!
HICCUP. ♪
SHUFF

SO THIS IS WHERE THE HUMAN WITH THE YO-KAI WATCH LIVES...
JINGLE

WELCOME HOME, DAD!
SHUFF
OH!
HEEE-EEEY. ♪
WHAAA
YO YO YO! WHAT'S UP, SON?! ♪
YOU WANT TO HANG OUT? ♪
OH YEAH! DAD IN THE HOUSE! IN THE HIZ-OUSE! ♪
SNAP
SNAP
SNAP
SNAP
...
OH YEAH!
WHAT?! IS HE HALF-ASLEEP?!
KREEEAK
MOM, DAD'S ACTING WEIRD...

WHAAAT?

HONEY?! DON'T YOU KNOW WHAT TIME IT IS?!

WHY ARE YOU SO LATE AND SO LOUD?

HEY! MOM'S BEING LOUD TOO!

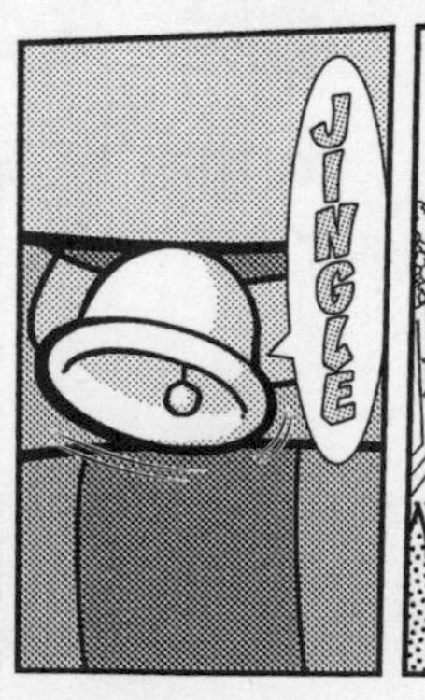

GOOD MORNING! ♪
!!!
HMM?
PFFFFFFT!!
HAHAHA
DO YOU GET IT?!
?
I JUST TOLD YOU "GOOD MORNING!"
HA HA HA!
But it's clearly nighttime!
HYUK! HYUK!
BAM BAM BAM
GREAT. ANOTHER WEIRD YO-KAI...
THIS IS A YO-KAI FROM BBQ.
WHAT?! I THINK USAPYON MEN-TIONED HE WAS FROM THAT AREA ONCE.
MEOW, MEOW, MEOW ...
BMP BMP BMP ♪
ALL RIGHT, EVERYBODY... MY NAME'S TOMNYAN! ♪
BMP BMP BMP
ARE YOU READY ?!
LET'S GO!
?

BMP BMP BMP BMP
I'M A COOL CAT YO-KAI FROM BBQ WHO WON'T EAT TACOS IN ANY SHAPE OR WAY!
... T-O-M-N-Y-A-N !!
THAT'S MY NAME! SAY IT WITH ME NOW! SAY, TOMNYAN!
COME ON! SAY IT!
BMP
...
BMP BMP
COME ON!
...
BMP BMP BMP
YEAH! SAY IT!
...
FWUMP
YOU'RE SUCH PARTY POOPERS!
I'M STILL GETTING A REAL APELICAN VIBE FROM HIM...
YOU'RE RIGHT. I CAN'T GET ONBOARD WITH HOW BOMBASTIC HE IS...
OH NO! THE PEOPLE HERE ARE...
...WITHDRAWN! SHY! LACKING IN CONVICTION! WITH NO OPINIONS OF THEIR OWN!
THEY SOLVE EVERYTHING WITH MONEY! AND THEY SHUN ANYONE DIFFERENT FROM THEM!
HE'S SO RUDE...

AAAHH!!
HOW COULD I FORGET?! TOM CAT SHOCK!!
CRYPTIC YO-KAI TOMNYAN
...
SIGH
PEOPLE HERE ARE SO DIFFERENT FROM WHAT I'M USED TO.
TOMMY SHOCK...?
WAS THAT...A SPECIAL MOVE OR SOME-THING?
WHAT DO YOU MEAN BY "PEOPLE HERE?"
ARE THINGS REALLY THAT DIF-FERENT AT BBQ?
...

HA HA HA HA HA

...?

I WANT TO BE YOUR FRIEND! ♪

FSH

OH, BUT... WHAT ABOUT MY QUES-TION? ARE THINGS REALLY THAT DIFFER-ENT?

IN RETURN, I'LL INTRODUCE YOU TO ALL KINDS OF YO-KAI FROM THE SAME PLACE AS ME! ♪

!!!

OH!

WAIT...I THINK I KNOW WHY HE'S BEING SO VAGUE!

THERE'S NO DOUBT ABOUT IT!

THAT MUST BE IT!
OKAY, LET'S FORGET ABOUT WHERE YOU COME FROM!
YEAH!
IT'S ONE OF THOSE THINGS THAT CAN'T BE EX-PLAINED!

"THINGS THAT CAN'T BE EXPLAINED" ARE POWERFUL FORCES THAT CANNOT BE SEEN OR DESCRIBED. IN THIS CASE, IT'S A PLOT POINT THAT AN "ORDINARY MANGA ARTIST" HAS NO POWER OVER!

!
!
SHFF

IT'S NICE TO MAKE NEW FRIENDS NO MATTER WHERE THEY COME FROM.
FSH
NICE TO MEET YOU.

YOU WANT... TO MEET... ME?!
WHAT?
NICE TO MEET YOU. ♪
OH ...
MEOW! I CAME HERE TO MAKE FRIENDS WITH LOCAL YO-KAI!

WOW! YOU'RE AN EXCELLENT JUDGE OF YO-KAI!

MAKE FRIENDS WITH ME AND YOU'LL BECOME FRIENDS WITH PRACTICALLY EVERY YO-KAI HERE!

OH YEAH!

TO TELL YOU THE TRUTH...

...BECAUSE OF ME, NATE ADAMS IS FRIENDS WITH TONS OF YO-KAI!

BAAM

RIGHT, NATE-DOG?!

WHAP

NATE-DOG?!

HE USED THE YO-KAI WATCH TO BECOME FRIENDS WITH YO-KAI...?! BUT OTHER HUMANS WOULD JUST USE IT TO "WATCH" THE YO-KAI...!
YOU'RE PROBABLY FROM THE SAME PLACE AS USAPYON! DO YOU KNOW HIM?
...
THERE'S... ALREADY A YO-KAI LIKE ME HERE?!
NO.
WE'LL INTRODUCE YOU TO HIM!
NO! I'D RATHER MEET YO-KAI THAT ARE FROM AROUND HERE! ♪
THEN LET'S START WITH JIBAN-YAN!
RIGHT!
CALL-ING JIBAN-YAN!

TIIING
WHAT ?!
JIBANYAN... WHAT HAPPENED ?!
SHUP
NATE... IT'S YOU...

AFTER ENDLESS, NEVER-ENDING BATTLES AGAINST YO-KAI...
I WAS IN DANGER OF FORGETTING MY REAL GOAL: **TO DEFEAT THE TRUCKS.**
!!!
TO TAKE A BETTER LOOK AT MYSELF, I BECAME BUDDHANYAN!

WAAAAAH

WHAT ?!

WHAT DID YOU JUST SAY ?!
I'M SICK AND TIRED OF NYAN YO-KAI!
NO, BE-FORE THAT! ABOUT THE TRUCKS!

I BECAME A YO-KAI BECAUSE I WANTED TO DEFEAT TRUCKS!
UNBELIEV-ABLE...

WHEN I, TOMYAN, WAS STILL A CAT...
A FLASHBACK SCENE... AND HE'S REFERRING TO HIMSELF IN THE THIRD PERSON ...?
MEOW.
I WAS A GENTLE PET, BELONGING TO A GIRL NAMED EMILY!
!!!
BUT ONE DAY...
COME ON, TOM-NYAN! ♪
MEOW!
WHAT...

IF ONLY I HAD BEEN STRONGER...

IF ONLY I HAD PUNCHED THE TRUCK AWAY...

THEN I WOULD NEVER..

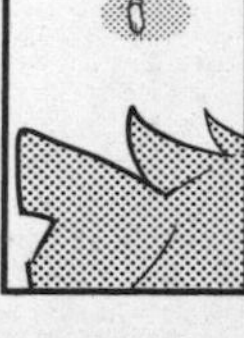

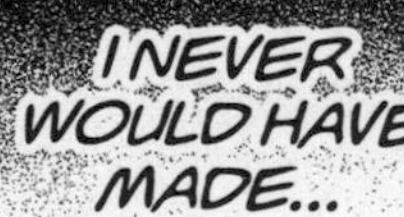
I NEVER WOULD HAVE MADE...

...EMILY CRY LIKE THAT—

I CAN'T BE-LIEVE IT...
HE'S JUST LIKE JIBAN-YAN...

?
THIS... ISN'T GOOD ...

NOT ONLY DOES HE LOOK LIKE ME WITH A SIMILAR NAME... BUT WE EVEN SHARE AN ORIGIN STORY!

THEY'RE FINALLY RUNNING OUT OF IDEAS!

AHHHHHH!

BAM

HE'S RIGHT...! SO FAR, HIS ABILITY WORKS THE SAME AS APELICAN'S!

WHAT DO YOU MEAN?

WELL, I...

IT'S AN IN-CREDIBLE COINCI-DENCE...!

IT'S HARD TO BELIEVE WE'RE DIFFERENT PEOPLE... I MEAN, CATS!

MEOW.

THE BEST
THE FISH PLACE
FISH
THIS IS THE INTERSECTION WHERE THE TRUCK GOT ME.
VRROOM
YOOOSH
HERE IT COMES! LET'S DO IT!
CHOOM CHOOM CHOOM CHOOM
I'LL BEAT THE TRUCK AND GO MEET AMY!
PAWS OF FURY!
GO!!
CHOOM CHOOM CHOOM CHOOM CHOOM CHOOM

HNNGH
SAME AS ALWAYS...
AH! HERE COMES ANOTHER ONE!
LOOK OUT, JIBANYAN!
VROOM
THESE TRUCKS ARE NOTHING COMPARED TO THE TRUCK THAT GOT ME!
TAKE THIS!!
LET'S HOPE HE'S RIGHT ...
TOMNYAN!

CENTI-
CUFFS!
CHOOM!!
CHOOM!! CHOOM!!
CHOOM!!
CHOOM!!
CHOOM!!
CHOOM!!
HOOM!!
BEST

TUNK
TUNK
TUNK
YOUR CAR GETTING MYSTERIOUS DENTS IS ALSO THE WORK OF A YO-KAI!
CHOOM
CHOOM
HE'S ACTUALLY DAMAGING IT!
HE'S SO POWER-FUL!
CHOOM
CHOOM
!!!
MEEEEOOOOOW!

KA-THUNK
THUNK
MEOW!!
IT STILL GOT HIM!
They're so alike!
HNNGH
URGH!!
ARE YOU ALL RIGHT?!
WHAAAAAA!
YOUR TRUCKS ARE SMALL...BUT POWERFUL...
I SHOULD HAVE... STUDIED MY OPPONENT MORE...
...
I DIDN'T EXPECT THIS

WHAAA!!
TOM CAT SHOCK!
I DON'T THINK THAT'S GOING TO CATCH ON...

TMP TMP...
VOOOOOOSH
VOOOOSH

VOOOOOSH
WHEEZE
WHEEZE
URRGH
GAAH
HE RAN OUT OF BREATH! THAT'S EVEN SADDER THAN GETTING HIT AGAIN!

...
I...
...
HE'S... JUST LIKE ME...
AND NO MATTER HOW HARD HE TRIES... HE CAN'T SUCCEED... HE'S JUST LIKE ME.
HE MADE HIS BELOVED CRY... THEN BECAME A YO-KAI BECAUSE HE FELT SO POWERLESS ...

WHAAAA

...NEVER KNEW I WAS THAT PATHETIC...

THAT'S WHAT UPSETS YOU?! YOU DON'T EMPATHIZE WITH HIM AT ALL?!

VRROOM
THUNGK
ARRRRGH!
HE WAS IN THE MIDDLE OF THE ROAD.
HE REALLY IS PATHETIC...

ARE YOU OKAY ...?
URGH ...
WUMPT

MY WIG IS RUINED!
THAT WAS A WIG...?

I HAD IT CUS-TOM MADE TOO ...
...

GAAAAH!
DON'T WORRY! YOU STILL LOOK THE SAME BECAUSE OF ALL THE BUMPS ON YOUR HEAD!
?
TOM-NYAN.
!!!
A HUMAN AND YO-KAI...BEING FRIENDS...
...

IF YOU WANT TO MAKE MORE FRIENDS HERE, I'LL INTRODUCE YOU TO THEM!
FOR SURE!
!!!
I SEE...

AS LONG AS I HAVE THIS HUMAN, I CAN USE THE POWERS OF ALL SORTS OF YO-KAI... WHAT A USEFUL FRIEND TO HAVE...
JINGLE

I NEVER THOUGHT OF THAT!

AH-HH

WHAT'S WRONG?

OH, NOTHING! ♪
NICE TO MEET YOU! ♪

I GOT ANOTHER YO-KAI MEDAL! ♪
PO
PT

LET'S TELL USAPYON ABOUT TOMNYAN! ♪
OKAY! ♪
COMING HERE WAS THE RIGHT DECISION.

SORRY, NATE ADAMS... SORRY, YO-KAI...
HEH HEH

YOU'RE ALL JUST PART OF MY PLAN!
FISH
NATE ADAMS'S CURRENT NUMBER OF YO-KAI FRIENDS: 65

CHAPTER 101:
I'VE BEEN INSPIRITED BY A FLOATING HEAD!
FEATURING WANDERING HEAD HELMSMAN

WHAAAAAA

THAT'S WHAT WE CALL A **GHOST**!

...JUST A **FLOATING HEAD YO-KAI** WHO'S BEEN SEPARATED FROM HIS BODY.

WANDERING HEAD

HELMSMAN

RRMBL...
SCARY...?
I'M LOOKING FOR A BODY LIKE THIS.
HAVE YOU SEEN IT?
A BODY LIKE THAT IS JUST WANDERING ABOUT?! SCARY!
REALLY? I GUESS THAT'S OKAY, THEN.
IT IS?!

SHUDDER
A FLOATING HEAD IS PRETTY SCARY TOO, YOU KNOW...!
TREMBLE
TREMBLE
OH, RIGHT. I GUESS A HEADLESS BODY STUMBLING AROUND IS PRETTY SCARY!
TREMBLE
TREMBLE

SHUPT
YAAAAH!
...
OH YEAH... HE CAN'T SEE...

YOU MUST HAVE BEEN A MIGHTY WARRIOR BEFORE YOU LOST YOUR HEAD...
OH NO, I JUST MISPLACED IT IN MY SLEEP.
ZUFF

I SEE...

WAIT A MINUTE! HOW DO YOU MISPLACE YOUR HEAD WHILE YOU'RE SLEEPING?!
HUFF HUFF
THAT'S EXACTLY WHAT I WANT TO KNOW!
SIGH... I ALMOST THOUGHT THAT HE WAS GOING TO HANDLE IT...

FORGET IT! I KNOW WHO CAN TAKE CARE OF THIS!
VNNN

YAAAAAAH!
SHOGUNYAN!
VRRRRNN
!!!
IT'S... IT'S...
...
IT'S BEEN A FEW CEN-TURIES SINCE WE LAST SAW EACH OTHER!
YOU KNOW EACH OTHER?!
...
IT'S YOU, LAST NYANMURAI!
NEVER THOUGHT I'D SEE YOU AGAIN...!

SLASH
SHOGUNYAAAAAAAN!
ARRRRRGH!
FWAP
...
THAT WAS DANGEROUS! IF I WASN'T A YO-KAI, IT MIGHT HAVE KILLED ME!
SORRY... YOU STARTLED ME.
YOU SHOULDN'T CHOP SOMEONE IN HALF JUST FOR STARTLING YOU!
LONG TIME NO SEE, SHOGUNYAN! HOW HAVE YOU BEEN?
OH NOT BAD!
WHOLE AGAIN.
HE'S A YO-KAI AND JUST GOT CUT IN HALF!
I SEE. YOU DIED GLORIOUSLY IN BATTLE, DEFENDING OUR LORD...
I... SURVIVED, HOWEVER...
...
SO I'M STILL HERE, WAITING...
TRAPPED WITH THE SHAME OF NOT HAVING SERVED MY LORD...
I UNDERSTAND. IT'S THE WAY OF THE SAMURAI.
NATE... CAN I ASK YOU FOR A FAVOR?
?

USE YOUR YO-KAI FRIENDS AND THEIR POWERS TO START A WAR!

GIVE HIM SOMETHING TO SACRIFICE HIMSELF FOR!

ZUFF

EHHH... THAT'S NOT REALLY WHAT I WANT...

WHAT A CRAZY THING TO ASK FOR!

TRYING TO FALL TO HIS KNEES!

I DON'T NEED TO SACRIFICE MYSELF...

...BUT AS A SAMURAI, I NEED SOMETHING TO LIVE FOR...A DUTY...OR CAUSE...

THEN LET'S BE LIKE SHOGUNYAN AND HELP PEOPLE AND YO-KAI IN TROUBLE!

...

IT'D BE REASSURING TO HAVE A FRIEND THAT'S AS STRONG AS YOU ARE! ♪
!!!

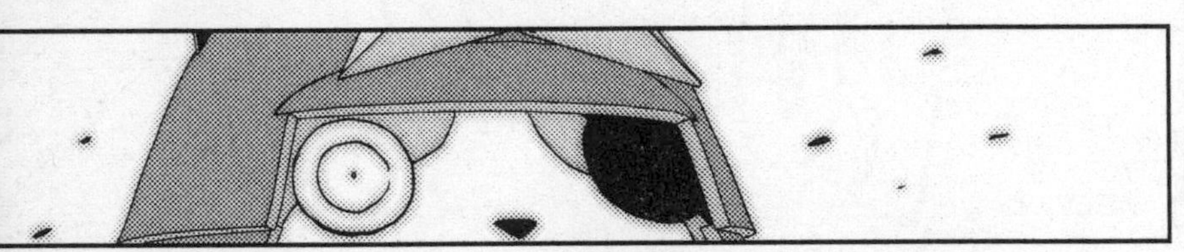

LAST NYANMURAI... IT'S SO REASSURING TO HAVE YOU BY MY SIDE!

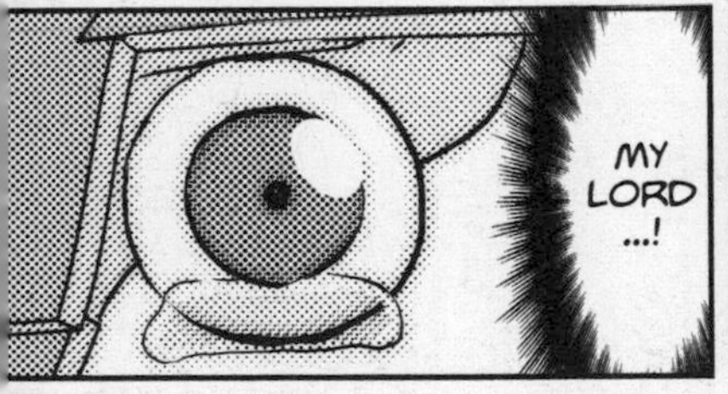
MY LORD ...!

THE FLOW OF TIME IS A TRAGIC THING, SHO-GUNYAN...
I JOURNEYED TO JAPAN, I LEARNED THE WAY OF THE SAMURAI AND WE TRAINED TOGETHER. THOSE WERE THE DAYS...

THEN LET'S WORK TOGETHER AGAIN, LAST NYAN-MURAI!
...
A SAMURAI MAY NOT HAVE MULTIPLE LORDS. I ONLY HAVE ONE AND IT IS HE THAT NAMED ME.

HOW-EVER...

...I CAN HELP YOU AS A FRIEND.

FSHooo

HURRAY! ♪

POPT

I GOT ANOTHER YO-KAI MEDAL! ♪

ALLOW ME TO INTRODUCE YOU TO SHOGUNYAN'S DESCENDANT...

...JIBANYAN!

THIS IS THE LAST NYANMURAI.

WHAAAAAAAAT?!

HUUUUUH

NOT ANOTHER NYAN YO-KAI...!

THERE'S SO MANY OF THEM...

OH COME ON...

AND THIS IS TOMNYAN!

NICE TO MEET YOU! ♪

...
?
YOU...
DID YOU THINK YOU COULD TRICK ME?!
WHAT?!
WHAT'S GOING ON?!
NATE ADAMS'S CURRENT NUMBER OF YO-KAI FRIENDS: 68

CHAPTER 107:
KNOCK SOME SENSE INTO THAT SLACKER!
FEATURING LAZY YO-KAI HORIZONTAIL
YOU CAN'T DECEIVE ME!
WHO ARE YOU REALLY?!

I'M NATE ADAMS. AN ORDINARY ELEMENTARY SCHOOL STUDENT.
WHAT IS HE TALKING ABOUT?!
EVER SINCE I GOT A YO-KAI WATCH, I'VE BEEN ABLE TO SEE YO-KAI.
I HAVE BEEN MEETING MORE YO-KAI FROM BBQ LATELY...
BMP BMP

A CRYPTIC CAT YO-KAI WHO LOOKS A LOT LIKE JIBANYAN...

TOM-NYAN.

AND A YO-KAI WHO HAS BEEN ALIVE SINCE TRAVELING TO JAPAN DURING THE WARRING STATES PERIOD...
LAST NYAN-MURAI.

YOUR ACCENT... I CAN TELL THERE'S SOME-THING OFF ABOUT IT!

AND THIS IS TOM-NYAN... HE'S FROM BBQ!

NICE TO MEET YOU! ♪

YOU'RE NOT FROM BBQ! I CAN TELL!

WHO ARE YOU AND WHERE DID YOU COME FROM?!

A WHILE BACK WE DECIDED TO JUST IGNORE THIS WHOLE ISSUE. IT'S ONE OF THOSE THINGS THAT JUST CAN'T BE EXPLAINED.
IT'S ONE OF THOSE THINGS THAT CAN'T BE EXPLAINED!
THAT MUST BE IT!!
OKAY, LET'S FORGET ABOUT WHERE YOU CAME FROM!
WHAAAT?! REALLY?!
THINGS THAT CAN'T BE EXPLAINED?!
"THINGS THAT CAN'T BE EXPLAINED" ARE POWERFUL FORCES THAT CANNOT BE SEEN OR DESCRIBED. IN THIS CASE, IT'S A PLOT POINT THAT AN "ORDINARY MANGA ARTIST" HAS NO POWER OVER!

WELL, IN THAT CASE...

I'LL ASK FOR FOR-GIVENESS.

PLEASE FORGIVE ME.

WOW!

WAIT, WAIT, WAIT!

FUSSSH

EXCELLENT.

MY PLAN REQUIRES STRONG YO-KAI LIKE HIM.

SAMURAI ALWAYS KEEP THEIR WORD, DON'T THEY? ♪

LAST NYANMURAI VALUES BUSHIDO, THE WAY OF THE SAMURAI.

THE WAY OF THE SAMURAI...

HMM...

GIVE ME A BREAK!

UGGGH...

LIKE... WHAT'S THE POINT OF THIS ANYWAY?!

WHAT?! WHAT'S WRONG?!

...

PEOPLE WILL COMPLAIN IF THIS STORY IS TOO VIOLENT!
WHAT ERA ARE YOU FROM? THIS IS SO OLD-SCHOOL AND INAPPROPRIATE.
OLD ...?
HEY!
SLASH

YOU WERE ASKING FOR IT, WHISPER.
ARE YOU ALL RIGHT?!
I CANNOT FORGIVE ANYONE WHO MOCKS THE WAY OF THE SAMURAI.
SWSH SWSH
A SAMURAI WON'T ATTACK AN UNARMED OPPONENT...
...BUT HIS DISHON-ORABLE WORDS COULDN'T GO UNPUN-ISHED!
CHIKT
TWITCH TWITCH

...
HUMPH...I WASN'T EXPECTING THAT!
WHAT?
PHEW! YOU'RE OKAY!
OWW.. HOW... COULD YOU...?

...
WHAT'S GOING ON?! IS THIS LAST NYANMURAI'S ABILITY?!
AIIIEEEEEE!
WHAT?! ANOTHER ME?!

ARRRRRGH!
NO! I'VE BEEN SLICED IN HALF!
I CAN'T EAT ANYTHING NOW BECAUSE IT'LL JUST FALL OUT!
THAT'S WHAT YOU'RE UPSET ABOUT?!
DASH
LAST NYAN-MURAI!
JIBANYAN'S MAD ABOUT WHAT HE DID TO WHISPER!
HOW COULD YOU DO THAT TO HIM?!
!!!
WUMPT
URGH...
WUMPT
!!!

OKAY... YO-KAI MEDAL!
I DON'T THINK JIBANYAN WILL BE MUCH HELP BUT...
...THIS YO-KAI MIGHT BE!
YO-KAI MEDAL, DO YOUR THING! CALLING...
KRRKT
VRRRN
MANJIMUTT!
GRRR! GRRR!
WHY DID YOU SUMMON ME IN THE MIDDLE OF THE NIGHT?!
WE'RE LOOKING FOR HIS HEAD!
ZZZooo ZZZooo
HIS HEAD?!
I WANT YOU TO FIND IT USING YOUR KEEN SENSE OF SMELL!
HA... THAT'S RIGHT...
BRILLIANT! A DOG'S SENSE OF SMELL IS A MILLION TIMES MORE SENSITIVE THAN A HUMAN'S!

BUT I'VE GOT A HUMAN HEAD, YOU KNOW...
AAAAAH!
YOU'RE RIGHT! THAT MEANS YOUR SENSE OF SMELL IS NO BETTER THAN MINE!
HUFF HUFF
SORRY
I KNOW! THERE'S ANOTHER YO-KAI THAT CAN HELP ME FIND IT EVEN MORE QUICKLY!
KRRKT
CALLING ...
... NOKO!!
VRRRRN
A YO-KAI THAT BRINGS LUCK TO PEOPLE IT INSPIRITS.

HNNNGH
NOOOO, NOT NOW!
I'm so unlucky!
TWITCH TWITCH
KWEEE... (SORRY...I USED UP MY POWERS...)
WHAAAAT?!
IT TURNS INTO A STRANGE CREATURE ONCE IT USES UP ITS LUCK POWER.
IT'S TOO DARK TO WALK AROUND LOOKING FOR IT...
WE NEED SOME AD-VANCED TECH-NOLOGY!
KRKRKT
ROBO-NYAN F!
FWAASH
JUST LEAVE IT TO ME!
I'LL SCAN THE ENTIRE TOWN FROM THE SKIES!
WHY ARE YOU JUST USING YOUR HEAD?
TO CONSERVE BATTERIES!
I SEE!
AH!
DID YOU FIND IT?!

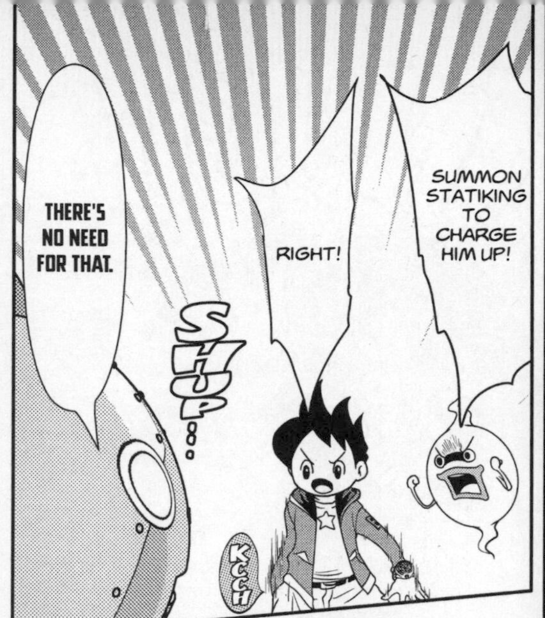
SUMMON STATIKING TO CHARGE HIM UP!
RIGHT!
THERE'S NO NEED FOR THAT.
SHUP...
KCCH

WHAT? ROBONYAN, I THOUGHT YOU WERE OUT OF BATTERIES...
HA...

I DON'T NEED BATTERIES ANYMORE.
YOU MEAN... YOU CAN GENERATE POWER ON YOUR OWN?!

NO! MY HEAD BATTERY RAN OUT!!
HEY!
FWEEEE
PSSH PSSH

STOP IT!
So it's you!
YOU STOLE HIS HEAD!
I'LL BE GOING NOW!
THANKS FOR EVERYTHING!

BWWWT...
I'M OUT OF BATTERIES...
VRRRN
STATIKING!
AGGGGH!
COME ON!
ZZZ...
ZZZT
ZZZT
LEAVE IT TO ME!
ARRRRRRGH!
ZZT
ZZZT ZZT
?
OOPS.
PSSSSH...
...
SORRY. IT'S A LONG STORY BUT ROBANYAN'S OVER THERE...
I'M SORRY!
I'LL REDO IT RIGHT AWAY!

KR-KSHOOM
BATTERY CHARGE COMPLETE!!
!!
ZHOOOOSH
NOOO-!!
CHOOOOM

FWOOOSH
ARRRRRRGH-!
HE WASN'T REALLY A BAD YO-KAI, BUT...
HE TOOK SOME-THING THAT DIDN'T BELONG TO HIM. IT HAD TO BE DONE.
EVER SINCE I LOST MY HEAD, I HAVEN'T BEEN ABLE TO THINK STRAIGHT... AND WHEN I TRY TO CONCENTRATE, I END UP FALLING ASLEEP...
DWOOM
I UNDER-STAND. ♪ I GET SLEEPY WHEN I DON'T UNDER-STAND MY SCHOOL-WORK!
...
BUT DON'T WORRY, I'LL LOOK FOR YOUR HEAD!
BUT WHY WOULD YOU HELP ME?
IT'S ONLY RIGHT TO HELP THOSE WHO ARE IN TROUBLE, WHETHER THEY'RE HUMAN OR YO-KAI.
...
THANK YOU.
FSH...
OOOH!

I GOT ANOTHER YO-KAI MEDAL. ♪
POPT

IT'S GOTTEN TOO LATE NOW, BUT I'LL HELP YOU LOOK TOMOR-ROW!
NO PROBLEM! SEARCH FOR IT WHEN YOU HAVE THE TIME. AND WHEN YOU FIND IT...

THE YO-KAI WAS TOUCHED BY NATE'S KINDNESS AND DECIDED TO BECOME HIS FRIEND.
I'LL NEVER GET TIRED OF IT.

...CALL ME UP WITH THAT MEDAL! ♪
AHHH...
ZZZ...
IS THAT WHY HE GAVE IT TO YOU?!
SO HE COULD GO TO SLEEP!
I can't believe I was touched by this!

OKAY... I'LL JUST LOOK FOR IT WHEN I FEEL LIKE IT.
SOUNDS GOOD TO ME.

?
NATE.
KA-SHK

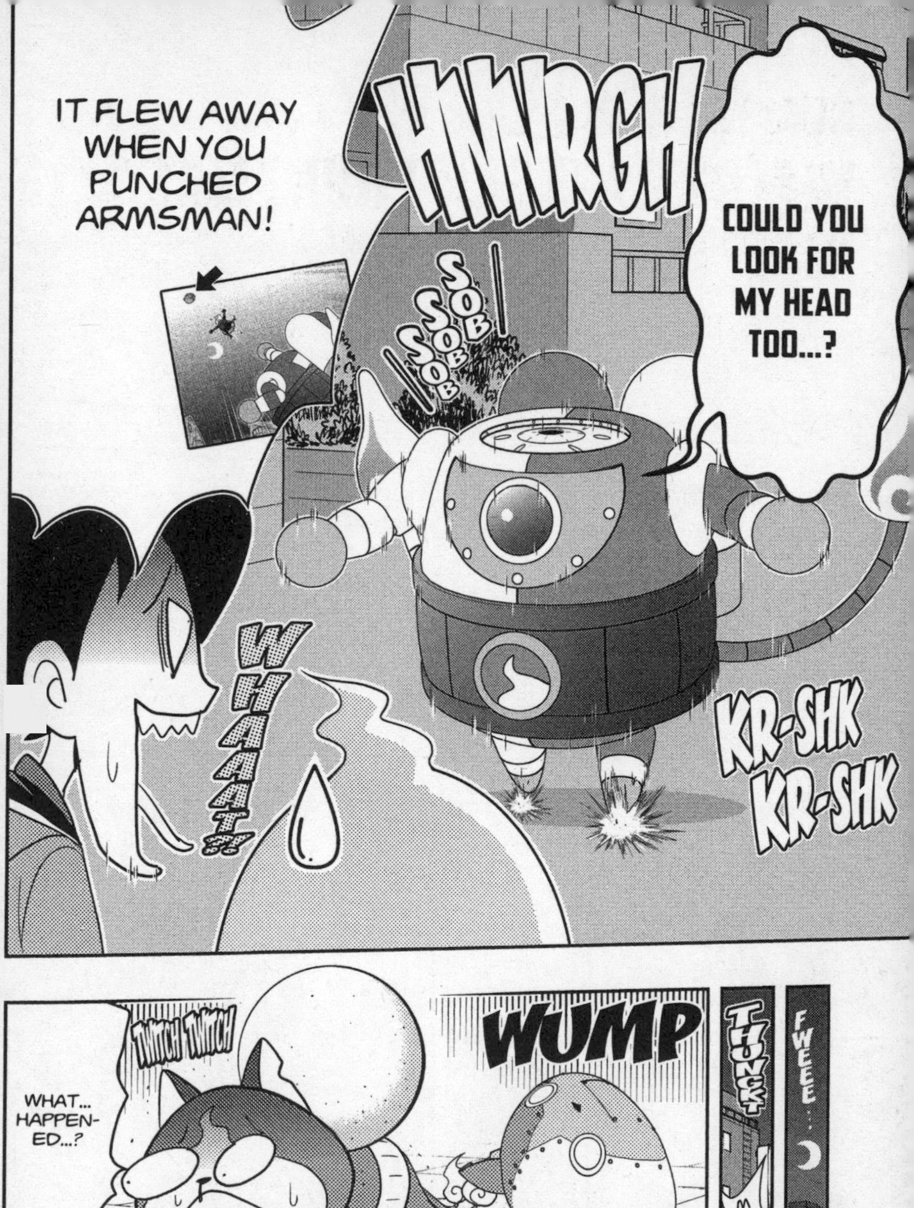

IT FLEW AWAY WHEN YOU PUNCHED ARMSMAN!

HNNRGH

SOB SOB SOB

COULD YOU LOOK FOR MY HEAD TOO...?

WHAAAAT?!

KR-SHK KR-SHK

WHAT... HAPPEN-ED...?
TWITCH TWITCH
WUMP
THUNCK
MEOW?!
FWEEE...

NATE ADAMS'S CURRENT NUMBER OF YO-KAI FRIENDS: 66

CHAPTER 105:
WATCH OUT! SAND DUNE BATTLE!
FEATURING SAND DUNE YO-KAI DANKE SAND

WHAAAAAA
YOU'RE HUGE! WERE YOU TRYING TO EAT ME?!
ZLUUUUUUSH
DON'T WORRY! I JUST NEED TO CLOSE MY MOUTH. ♪ BUT FIRST, ALLOW ME TO INTRODUCE MYSELF! MY NAME IS—
NO! CLOSE YOUR MOUTH FIRST!
OKEY-DOKE.
CHOMPT
ARRRRGH! YOUR TEETH! YOUR TEETH!
WHOOPS.

I'M NOT A PICKY EATER THOUGH, SO I EAT SNAKES, FROGS, BIRDS, INSECTS... PRETTY MUCH WHATEVER COMES MY WAY! ♪
DANKE FOR SEAFOOD!
SORRY ABOUT THAT! I KEEP MY MOUTH OPEN SO I CAN LIVE OFF THE FISH AND CRABS THAT FALL IN! ♪
HEH HEH
I...DIDN'T NEED TO KNOW THAT PART...
HEFH HEFH
SAND DUNE YO-KAI
DANKE SAND
WOW! ♪ ALL THIS TALK ABOUT FOOD IS MAKING ME HUNGRY! ♪
GRRUMBLE
...
HMM?
...
?
MMMM
I HEARD THAT! YOU'RE DROOL-ING JUST LOOK-ING AT ME!
DANKE FOR COMING BY!
MAYBE I'LL EAT YOU AFTER ALL! ♪
YOU EAT OTHER YO-KAI?! THAT'S HORRIBLE! YOU WON'T MAKE A MEAL OUT OF ME THOUGH!
ZSSSSSH
PAWS OF FURY!
CHOOM CHOOM
CHOOM CHOOM CHOOM CHOOM

BOOF
BOOF
BOOF
BOOF
MY ATTACKS DON'T WORK BECAUSE HE'S MADE OF SAND!
HA HA HA HA. ♪
BOOF
BOOF
ZSSSSH
OH NO, YOU DON'T! I CONTROL ALL THE SAND HERE!
DASH
LUCKILY THE OCEAN IS RIGHT THERE!
FSSSHHH
I KNOW! I'LL HARDEN YOU WITH WATER AND SMASH YOU LIKE I DID WITH SAND-MEH!!
ZUFF
ZUFF
ZUFF
ZUFF
I'LL JUST DIG A HOLE THROUGH IT!

BWOOSH
ARRRRRGH!
HA HA HA. ♪ YOU CAN'T DIG A TUNNEL THROUGH DRY SAND! ♪
SHU-UPT
GAAAAAAH!
ECCHT! I GOT SAND IN MY MOUTH!
PTOOIE PTOOIE
GROSS! DON'T SPIT ON MY BODY!
THAT'S IT! I'LL MAKE YOU HARDEN BY SPITTING ON YOU!
PTOOIE PTOOIE PTOOIE PTOOIE PTOOIE PTOOIE
FIVE MINUTES LATER—
...
PTOOIE PTOOIE
...
PTOOIE PTOOIE
FWUMPT
IT'S NOT WORKING...
IF I CAN'T USE SEAWATER OR SPIT ON YOU, I'LL *PEE* ON YOU!
!!!
THAT'S DISGUSTING! STOP IT!
TAKE THIS!
SHWAA

AAAAH! I PEED TOO HARD!
SHWEEEEEEEE
SHOOOOOM
HUUUH?
WHAT?

...
SPLOOOSH

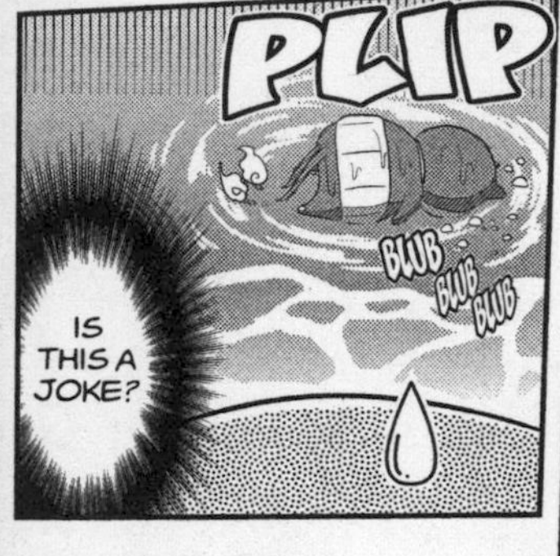

PLIP
BLUB BLUB BLUB
IS THIS A JOKE?

LET'S EAT! ♪
DANKE!
SPLUUB
MEOW ...

BURP

PSSSSHHHT
KRRRKT
ARR-RGH...!
HAVE A DRINK, ON ME!
!!!
MEOW-HA HA HA. ♪ I DID IT! ♪
O-OH NO...!!
CHOOM
CHOOM
NOW THAT YOU'RE ALL WET... PAWS OF FURY!
MEOW MEOW MEOW MEOW!
CHOOM
AGGGGH!
CHOOM
KRRRRAKT
PLIPT
PLIPT
ARRRRGH!
PLIPT
NSSSHH
OKAY... I GIVE UP...
OH? HE'S GONE...
OVER HERE!
I CAN'T MOVE UNTIL I'VE DRIED OUT...
UGH...
I'M A GENIUS! I RULE! I'M THE BEST AROUND!
I DID IT!

HMM?
TWITCH TWITCH
HELP... ME...
MY BODY IS CRUSHING HIM!
I GOT SWALLOWED UP BY SAND AFTER ALL...
HMMPH...
EVEN WHEN YOU THINK YOU'VE WON, DON'T GET COCKY!

CHAPTER 106:

A SORE LOSER YO-KAI

FEATURING IMPATIENT YO-KAI K'MON-K'MON

TOO SLOW!

I'M NATE ADAMS.

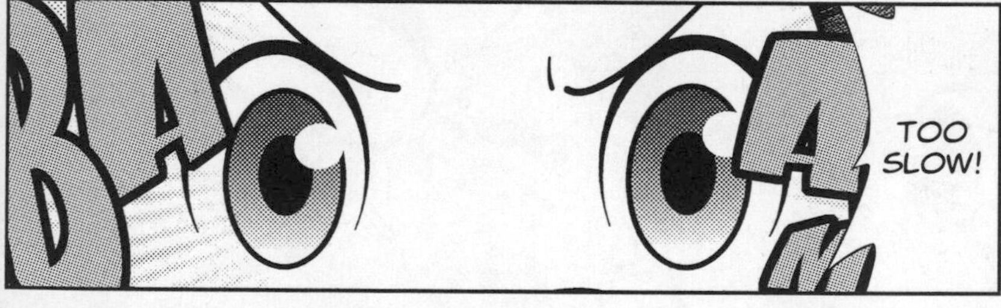
TOO SLOW!

TOO SLOW!
AN ORDINARY ELEMENTARY SCHOOL STUDENT.

SHF
SHF
SHF
SHF
I'M SUCH A SLOW WALK-ER!
SHF
SHF
WHY DON'T YOU JUST RUN?
SHF
SHF
IF I RAN, I'D GET WORN OUT...
SHF
SHF
SHF
...THEN I'D HAVE TO WASTE TIME WAITING TO CATCH MY BREATH!
WALKING FAST IS BEST BECAUSE I CAN DO IT CONSIS-TENTLY!
SHF
SHF
SHF
SHF
SHF
SHF
WAIT... WHY ARE YOU IN SUCH A HURRY?
I'M GETTING OLDER BY THE SECOND! I ONLY HAVE SO MUCH TIME!
TIME SPENT MOVING AROUND IS TIME WASTED, SO THE FASTER I MOVE THE BETTER!
SHF
SHF
SHF
SHF
IN MY OPINION, TIME SPENT WALKING AROUND IS AN OPPORTUNITY FOR SOME SERIOUS "ME TIME."
YOU CAN BE ALONE WITH YOUR THOUGHTS, CENTER YOURSELF, MAKE PLANS FOR THE REST OF THE DAY!

SHF SHF SHF SHF

LOOK OVER HERE! I'M TRYING TO DRAMATICALLY REVEAL MYSELF!

FWAASH

YO-KAI ARE INVISIBLE UNTIL THE YO-KAI WATCH SHINES ON THEM.

FWAASH

...

FWAASH

...

ARRRRGH! I CAN'T WAIT ANY LONGER! I'LL JUMP IN THE PATH OF THE WATCH'S LIGHT!

VOOOSH

FWAASH

VOOOSH

WHOA!

IT'S ME! ME! ME!

THUNGKT

VROOM

...

ARRRRRGH!

YO-KAI ARE INVISIBLE TO PEOPLE WHO DON'T HAVE THE YO-KAI WATCH.

...
NNNGH
TWITCH

!!!
NATE, BE CARE- FUL!
THAT'S ...!
ARE YOU OKAY?
TWITCH
HEY! I KNOW HIM!

MY NAME'S **K'MON-K'MON!**

I'M A YO-KAI THAT **HATES WAITING!**

...

IMPATIENT YO-KAI
K'MON-K'MON

I'M NOT GOING TO JUST SIT HERE AND WAIT FOR YOUR LOUSY EXPLANATION!

WHAAAAA?!

MY EXPLANATIONS ARE LOUSY?!

IT'S A BUTLER'S JOB TO ALWAYS PROVIDE HIS MASTER WITH THE MOST CORRECT AND DETAILED INFORMATION!

EXPLANATIONS ARE MY SPECIALITY!

HEH.

NOW YOU'RE GOING TO TELL ME YOU THOUGHT THAT WAS "LOUSY" RIGHT?! AND MAKE A FUNNY FACE?!

THAT'S WHAT ALWAYS HAPPENS IN A GAG MANGA, RIGHT?!

FWEEE
THEY'RE GONE...
I KNOW!
I COULDN'T WAIT FOR HIM TO STOP TALKING.
SHUFF
SHUFF
SHUFF
SHUFF
HEY! QUIT INSPIRIT-ING ME!
COME ON! WE'VE GOT TO GET HOME.
"GET HOME?!" YOU'RE TALKING ABOUT *MY* HOME!
SHUFF
SHUFF
SHF
SHF
SHUFF
THERE'S ONLY ONE YO-KAI WHO CAN DEAL WITH AN IRRITATED YO-KAI LIKE YOU!
?!
KRRK
CALLING HAPPIERRE!
VRRRRRN
...

HAPPI-URRGH!
KRAKT!
HUUUUUURGH!
YOU CAN'T ATTACK WHILE THEY'RE STILL BEING SUMMONED! THAT'S NOT FAIR!
TWITCH TWITCH
I COULDN'T WAIT FOR THE ENEMY TO COME OUT!
VNNNNNN
CALLING...
NATE, ARE YOU ALL RIGHT?
I'M OKAY. AND I HAVE JUST THE GUY FOR AN IMPATIENT YO-KAI LIKE THAT!
SHF SHF
SEE YA.
I DON'T HAVE TIME FOR YOUR COMPLAINTS.
HE'S SO IMPATIENT I CAN'T EVEN TALK TO HIM!
SHF SHF

HMMMM

CUTTA-NAH! GO GET—... HUH?!

CUTTA-NAH!

NNNGH

HE ALREADY LEFT.

NO !!!

LAZY YO-KAI CUTTA-NAH

HUH?

THP THP THP

WHAT AM I DOING ...

I KNEW IT...

NO CAN DO.

PICK PICK

CUTTA-NAH! HELP ME FIND HIM!

WHY AREN'T YOU COMING AFTER ME?!
I COULDN'T KEEP WAITING, SO I CAME BACK!
DO YOU WANT TO FIGHT US OR NOT?!
WHAAAAAAAAA
CLOMPT
CLOMPT
VOOSH
PLEASE ...
CALLING JIBANYAN!
VNNNNN

BLEEEEGH

WHAT HAPPENED TO YOU THIS TIME?

BURP.

VOOOOSH
I'LL TAKE CARE OF HIM!
THANKS!

SHF
SHF
I WANT YOU TO TEACH THIS GUY—... HEY! HE'S GOING HOME AGAIN!
I'M NOT GOING TO WAIT FOR-EVER!
SHF

I HAD TO DRINK... BURP... SEA-WATER BECAUSE OF... BURP... REASONS ....
PLIP
WHAT-EVER IT WAS, YOU'VE HAD TOO MUCH!
You're burping instead of saying "meow!"

CLOMPT CLOMPT
CLOMPT
CLOMPT

HE'S SO SLOW!

SLOSH
SLOSH

I CAN'T WAIT FOR YOU TO CATCH UP WITH ME!

KR
AKT

JIBANYAN!

!

SPLOOOOOSH

THE KICK MADE HIM COUGH UP ALL THE SEAWATER...!

HE DID DRINK A LOT, AFTER ALL...

RRMMLB

UNFOR-TUNATELY, YOU'RE WRONG!

UNNNNNGH

TWITCH

TWITCH

NOW'S YOUR CHANCE, JIBANYAN! FINISH HIM!

WHAA
I CAN'T DO THAT.

!!!

WHY? IS IT BECAUSE HE CAN'T MOVE?

I SEE! YOU WANT TO FIGHT FAIR!

NO...I JUST HAVEN'T STOPPED PUKING...
HEY...
BARRRRRF

HOW DARE YOU! NOW YOU'LL SUFFER AS I HAVE!
?!
VNNNNN

SPINNING PUKE SPLASH!
AGGGGH!
ZWOOOOOSH
CLOMP-CLOMP
ZWOOSH
UNNNGH! THAT'S DISGUST-ING!
BARRRRRF
WHY ARE YOU RUNNING ?!
IT'S ALL YOUR PUKE!
ZWOOSH
HEY! HOLD IT!
HE'S A YO-KAI WHO CAN'T WAIT!
SHU
TP...
!!!
HE WAITED ...!
URRRGH, I FEEL DIZZY...
NOW YOU'RE THROWING UP TOO?!

WUMPT

NNNGH... I'M DIZZY...

HE WORE HIMSELF OUT!

IT'S NOT RIGHT TO ATTACK HIM WHILE HE'S DOWN, SO LET'S WAIT.
OKAY.
...

VSSH
...
...

I'VE BEEN DEFEATED.

?!

I WON'T ACCEPT ANY PITY. I FORCED YOU TO...WAIT FOR ME DURING A BATTLE.

HUH. ♪

I THOUGHT YOU WERE REALLY ANNOYING...
...BUT YOU'RE JUST A YO-KAI WHO'S TRUE TO HIS WORD! YOU ADMITTED DEFEAT FOR "MAKING SOMEONE WAIT!"
...

BUT I WON'T BE YOUR FRIEND.
BEING FRIENDS INEVITABLY LEADS TO WAITING FOR THEM. I WON'T HAVE IT.
WAITING JUST MEANS THAT YOU NEED THEIR HELP. IT'S NOT A BAD THING!

REALLY?! I DON'T GET IT!
WELL ...

...I GUESS I'LL JUST WAIT FOR THE DAY YOU DECIDE TO BE MY FRIEND. ♪
!!!
HA! YOU GOT ME!

YOU FORCED ME TO MAKE YOU WAIT AGAIN!

FSH...

HA HA. ♪

NNNNNNGH
THERE'S NOTHING LEFT IN ME...
DON'T DRINK SALT WATER!
FWOOOO
YOU THREW UP TOO MUCH!
NATE ADAMS'S CURRENT NUMBER OF YO-KAI FRIENDS: 67

CHAPTER 105:
RETRIEVE THE PRECIOUS WATER!
FEATURING KAPPA YO-KAI WALKAPPA
IT...IT'S SCORCHING OUT...I'M SO... THIRSTY...
UNNNH
WATER... PLEASE...
UNNNH
MEOW? SOME-ONE'S COLLAPSED...!
TWITCH TWITCH
DID HE PASS OUT FROM THE HEAT?!
NNNGH...
HEY! ARE YOU ALL RIGHT?!
WATER... PLEASE...
I KNEW IT!
YOU HAVE A WATER BOTTLE ON YOU!
HERE WE GO...
SQUEE SQUEE

GLUG GLUG
GULP GULP
YOU'RE DRINKING MY WATER!
HEY! HEY!

OH! I FOR-GOT ABOUT YOU!
AH-HA!
WHAAAT?!
SO QUICK-LY?!
I WAS WOKEN UP FROM THE SHOCK!
I WAS SO WORRIED ABOUT YOU! ♪
SAVE IT!
WELL, I'M GLAD YOU'RE OKAY AT LEAST.
HERE YOU GO.
I BLACKED OUT FROM THE HEAT. I NEED WATER DESPER-ATELY...

WHAA-AAT?! IT'S EMPTY!
ACCCCCH!
THERE'S NOTHING LEFT! HOW COULD YOU?!
SHFF
SHFF
I GUESS I DRANK TOO MUCH...
WAY TOO MUCH!

HOW COULD YOU!
I'M... REALLY SORRY...

AWW...
IT LOOKS LIKE HE FEELS REALLY BAD...I GUESS I'LL FORGIVE HIM...

BUURP! I DRANK TOO MUCH!
UGH... SO FULL...
YOU DON'T EVEN FEEL BAD ABOUT WHAT YOU DID!

SORRY... I'LL MAKE IT UP TO YOU...
SNIFF
OKAY. GET ME SOME WATER AND I'LL FORGIVE YOU.

URRRGH
HURGH.
SPLOSH
SPLOSH
WHAT?! YOU'RE THROWING UP INTO MY WATER BOTTLE?!
THAT'S DISGUST-ING! I'LL NEVER FORGIVE YOU NOW!

ARRRRRGH... ALL THIS SHOUTING IS MAKING MY PLATE EVEN MORE DRY!
YOUR PLATE?

BLAAM
I'M WALKAPPA, A YO-KAI THAT TRAVELS IN SEARCH OF CLEAN WATER!
WAIT...SO DO YOU INSPIRIT PEOPLE OR NOT?
I DON'T INSPIRIT ANYONE BUT...
KAPPA YO-KAI **WALKAPPA**

MAYBE THE PEOPLE YOU INSPIRIT **GO BALD?**
I'M NOT BALD! OPEN YOUR EYES!
I'VE GOT A PLATE ON MY HEAD!
I SEE THE PLATE...BUT I STILL DON'T GET IT?

WE KAPPA DON'T GET THIRSTY, BUT WE DIE IF OUR PLATE DRIES OUT!
I USE THE WATER IN THAT BOTTLE TO KEEP MY PLATE FROM DRYING OUT! THAT'S WHY IT'S SO IMPORTANT!

GLUG GLUG
AHHH... I SEE.
BUT YOU'RE DRINKING IT AGAIN!
AND EVEN WORSE... THAT'S WATER THAT YOU JUST THREW UP!
I'VE HAD ENOUGH!
I'LL TEACH YOU THE FRIGHT-ENING STRENGTH AND POWER OF WATER!
OH YEAH?! YOU WANT A PIECE OF ME?!
ZUFF
BUT...MY PLATE HAS DRIED OUT AND I'M RUNNING LOW ON ENERGY, SO I'LL HAVE TO USE... **SOULTIMATE**!

HE'S GOING GET A TASTE OF MY MEGA WATERFALL!

ZWOOOSH

I GATHER UP WATER FROM THE WORLD AROUND ME AND SEND IT CRASHING DOWN ON MY ENEMIES! IT'S MY BIGGEST MOVE...!

SHARE YOUR WATER WITH ME!

VSH

SKY! EARTH! LIVING CREATURES FAR AND WIDE!

WUMPT
?

HNNGH
HIS PLATE DRIED OUT...

HEEEY!
YOU DIDN'T EVEN USE SOUL-TIMATE!

URGH... Water... please...
HMPH
FOR CRY-ING OUT LOUD...

SHWAAA
!!
YOU'RE SHARING WATER... WITH YOUR ENEMY...? YOU REALLY ARE...A NICE GUY...
Wait... you said you... didn't have... any left...?

ARRRGH! STOPPIT!
URRRGH!!
SHWAAA

YO-KAI FUNNIES!

UNNNH UNNNH
I HAVE TO GET... TO THE WATER... QUICKLY ...!
HEFH HEFH ...

SPLISH SPLISH
AHHHH. I FEEL ALIVE!

IT'S SUCH A NICE DAY OUT!
I'M GOING TO TAKE A NAP IN THE SUN!

AN HOUR LATER ...
SSSSSSSH
HIS PLATE DRIED OUT.

CHAPTER 106:
THE WAY OF THE SAMURAI
FEATURING SAMURAI YO-KAI LAST NYANMURAI

AAAAAAAH
THE WARRING STATES PERIOD OF JAPAN!
A TIME WHEN MAJOR BATTLES WERE FOUGHT BY SWORD-WIELDING SAMURAI!
HEFH HEFH
IT'S OVER...
OUR ARMY HAS BEEN DEFEATED ...
WE'RE THE ONLY TWO LEFT...
IT'S TIME....
ARE YOU GIVING UP, SHOGUN-YAN?!
ZUF
WE HAVE BUT A SINGLE OPTION. SURVIVE THIS SIEGE, REBUILD OUR ARMY AND RETALIATE.
!!!
NO...

AH
NO, NO, NO, NO!!
Look around us!
WE'RE TRAPPED!
IF BUT TWO RETAINERS WERE TO CUT DOWN 30,000 SOLDIERS, OUR LORD'S NAME WOULD NEVER BE FORGOT-TEN.
I SEE... THIS WOULD BE OUR FINAL SERVICE TO HIM.
LET'S GO!
I'LL SEE YOU AGAIN IN THE AFTERLIFE!
YAAA

YAAAA
THEY HAVE US COMPLETELY SURROUNDED!
And there are 30,000 of them!
PRESENT DAY
HEY, HAVE YOU HEARD?

THE GHOST OF A SWORD-WIELDING SAMURAI IS SAID TO APPEAR IN THE MOUNTAIN BEHIND SCHOOL.

...!!!

I'M SHOCKED THAT YOU AREN'T EMBARRASSED TO TALK ABOUT GHOSTS AND SPIRITS IN THIS DAY AND AGE!

HAVEN'T WE TALKED ABOUT THIS BEFORE?
THAT WAS WHEN SHOGUNYAN APPEARED...!
SEE VOLUME 2

BUT I'VE ACTUALLY SEEN YO-KAI BEFORE!
OH MAN, DON'T GET HIM GOING ABOUT YO-KAI AGAIN.
WHAT DO YOU THINK, NATE? GHOSTS EXIST, RIGHT?!

LOOK WHO'S TALKING!
WHAT? YOU DON'T BELIEVE IN GHOSTS? ARE YOU STUPID OR SOMETHING?!

A CAT YO-KAI, IN FACT!

WAIT... FOR REAL?
A CAT YO-KAI, HUH?
YUP. HIS NAME IS JIBANYAN AND HE'S A PRETTY NICE GUY.

A CAT YO-KAI?! WE WERE TALKING ABOUT SAMURAI GHOSTS!
WHATEVER. IT'S ALL MADE UP ANYWAY.
スタ スタ
THEY THINK GHOSTS ARE SPOOKY, NATE! THEY DON'T WANT TO HEAR ABOUT JIBANYAN!
BUT...
BEARS 90

I'VE MET TONS OF YO-KAI THAT ARE SCARIER LOOKING THAN GHOSTS. *And all of them are my pals!*

...I'M SO OVER GHOSTS. TALKING ABOUT THEM IS A WASTE OF TIME!

HMPH HMPH

TMP TMP TMP

KLAK KLAK KLAK

HE'S GOTTEN SO USED TO ALL OF THIS!

WELL...
5-2
...THAT GHOST IN THE MOUNTAIN ACTUALLY SOUNDS PRETTY INTERESTING.
IT'S PROBABLY JUST ARMSMAN.
MAYBE IT'S HIM SLEEPWALKING... OR MAYBE NOT.
FINE... LET'S GO CHECK IT OUT ON THE WAY HOME.
OKAY!

WOW, THIS MOUNTAIN IS HUGE...

I DON'T KNOW IF WE'LL EVER—

FUU FUU

SLAASH

THOOM
WOW...! HE CHOPPED DOWN THAT MASSIVE TREE WITH A SINGLE BLOW...!
MY SWORD IS AS SHARP AS EVER.
CHIK
BUT I...
...
LOOK OUT!

...AM STARV-ING...!

THAT'S NOT HIM! WHO IS IT?!

GRRUMBLE

MNNGH MNNGH

WHAT?!

I JUMPED TOO HIGH! HELP ME!
FWOOOOO
WHAT?!
HIS VERTICAL LEAP IS INCREDIBLE!
HOW FAR DID HE GO?!
And who is he anyway...?
?!
I'VE BEEN WAITING FOR YOU!
UP HERE!
WHAAAA
HE'S FLOATING?!
EH-HEH-HEH...

NNNNNNGH
I'M STUCK IN THIS TREE! HELP ME DOWN!
SSSH SSSH
...
KRCHK
PHEW... THANK YOU VERY MUCH. I AM IN YOUR DEBT.
AND NOW... TO FINISH THIS!
WHAT?! THAT DOESN'T MAKE ANY SENSE!
WHAAAT?! YOU'RE A SAMURAI FROM THE WARRING STATES PERIOD?!
WELL...I GUESS IT'S POSSIBLE FOR A YO-KAI...
DO YOU HAVE ANYTHING TO EAT?
GRRUMBLE
I'VE SURVIVED ON NOTHING BUT GRASS FOR THE LAST FEW HUNDRED YEARS.
GRASS?!
AHHHHH
I'VE GOT SOME LEFTOVER BREAD FROM LUNCH...
IT IS THE WAY OF THE SAMURAI TO REPAY ALL DEBTS FOR FOOD AND LODGING...
IT'S OKAY, DON'T WORRY ABOUT IT! ♪
...
MNCH MNCH MNCH

OF COURSE NOT! DID YOU EXPECT ME TO GIVE YOU SOMETHING IN RETURN FOR SUCH A MEASLY MEAL?!

AND WHAT IS THIS STUFF ANYWAY?! IT'S TOO FLUFFY!

THIS GUY'S REALLY SOME-THING...

HE LOOKS A LOT LIKE SHOGU-NYAN...
...MAYBE THEY'RE CON-NECTED SOME-HOW...?
He's eating grass...
I GUESS IT'S GRASS AGAIN TODAY...
MNCH MNCH
CHOMP CHOMP
SHFF SHFF
SHOULD WE ASK SHOGUN-YAN?

ZUFF
I'M FINALLY FULL.
!!!
ALLOW ME TO PROP-ERLY IN-TRODUCE MYSELF. I AM...

FROM TODAY ONWARD, YOU SHALL BE CALLED THE LAST NYANMURAI!

YES, MY LORD!

...A YO-KAI THAT BECAME A SAMURAI DURING THE WARRING STATES PERIOD.

I WAS MY LORD'S LAST LOYAL SAMURAI, SO HE NAMED ME THE **LAST NYANMURAI!**

SAMURAI YO-KAI **LAST NYANMURAI**

LAST NYAN-MURAI?!
THAT'S A COOL NAME!
I'VE MADE A DECISION... I'D LIKE TO REPAY YOU FOR THAT MEAGER MEAL YOU FED ME...
OH! YOU'LL BECOME MY FRIEND?!
AH...A FRIEND...
THAT BRINGS BACK MEMORIES... BUT **NO.**
WHAT?

WHAAAAA
I WILL BECOME YOUR RETAINER...IF YOU'RE ABLE TO DEFEAT ME!
WHAT?! WHAT ARE YOU TALKING ABOUT?! NO THANK YOU!
That makes no sense!
SSHHHHNG

VOOOOSH
AND IF I WIN...YOU'LL BE MY RETAINER!
LET'S BEGIN!
AGGGGGH
WHAAT?! WHAT HAPPENED TO REPAYING YOUR DEBTS?!

NATE, HURRY UP AND CALL SOMEONE WHO CAN FIGHT!
OKAY, FINE! I KNOW JUST THE YO-KAI FOR THE JOB!

VNNNNNNN
CALLING...

ARMSMAN!
YAAAAAH!
!!!
GRRAAAAH!
WOOOOSH

SHUPT

YAAAAH!

...

OH YEAH... HE CAN'T SEE...

YOU MUST HAVE BEEN A MIGHTY WARRIOR BEFORE YOU LOST YOUR HEAD...

ZUFF

OH NO, I JUST MISPLACED IT IN MY SLEEP.

I SEE...

WAIT A MINUTE! HOW DO YOU MISPLACE YOUR HEAD WHILE YOU'RE SLEEPING?!
HUFF HUFF
THAT'S EXACTLY WHAT I WANT TO KNOW!
SIGH... I ALMOST THOUGHT THAT HE WAS GOING TO HANDLE IT...

FORGET IT! I KNOW WHO CAN TAKE CARE OF THIS!
VNNN

SHOGUNYAN!
YAAAAAAH!
VRRRRNN
!!!
IT'S... IT'S...
IT'S YOU, LAST NYANMURAI!
NEVER THOUGHT I'D SEE YOU AGAIN...!
...
YOU KNOW EACH OTHER?!
IT'S BEEN A FEW CEN-TURIES SINCE WE LAST SAW EACH OTHER!
...

SLA
ASH
ARRRRRGH!
SHOGUNYAAAAAAAAN!
FWAP
THAT WAS DANGEROUS! IF I WASN'T A YO-KAI, IT MIGHT HAVE KILLED ME!
...
SORRY... YOU STARTLED ME.
YOU SHOULDN'T CHOP SOMEONE IN HALF JUST FOR STARTLING YOU!
LONG TIME NO SEE, SHOGUNYAN! HOW HAVE YOU BEEN?
OH NOT BAD!
WHOLE AGAIN.
HE'S A YO-KAI AND JUST GOT CUT IN HALF!
I SEE. YOU DIED GLORIOUSLY IN BATTLE, DEFENDING OUR LORD...
I... SURVIVED, HOWEVER...
...
SO I'M STILL HERE, WAITING...
TRAPPED WITH THE SHAME OF NOT HAVING SERVED MY LORD...
I UNDERSTAND. IT'S THE WAY OF THE SAMURAI.
NATE... CAN I ASK YOU FOR A FAVOR?
?

USE YOUR YO-KAI FRIENDS AND THEIR POWERS TO START A WAR!

GIVE HIM SOME-THING TO SAC-RIFICE HIMSELF FOR!

EHHH... THAT'S NOT REALLY WHAT I WANT...

WHAT A CRAZY THING TO ASK FOR!

ZUFF

TRYING TO FALL TO HIS KNEES!

I DON'T NEED TO SACRIFICE MYSELF...

...BUT AS A SAMURAI, I NEED SOMETHING TO LIVE FOR...A DUTY...OR CAUSE...

THEN LET'S BE LIKE SHOGUNYAN AND HELP PEOPLE AND YO-KAI IN TROUBLE!
...

IT'D BE REASSURING TO HAVE A FRIEND THAT'S AS STRONG AS YOU ARE! ♪
!!!

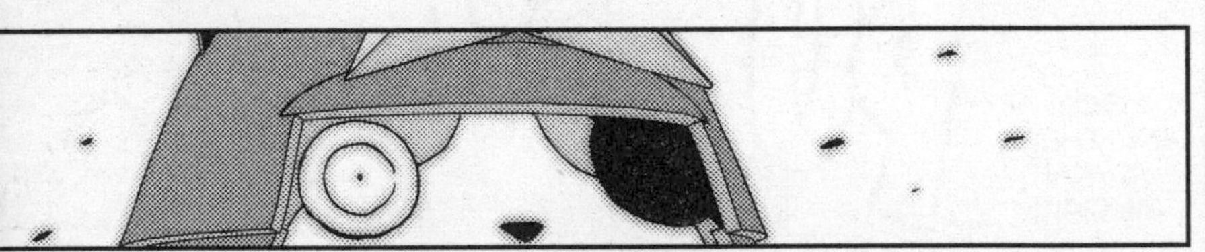

LAST NYANMURAI... IT'S SO REASSURING TO HAVE YOU BY MY SIDE!

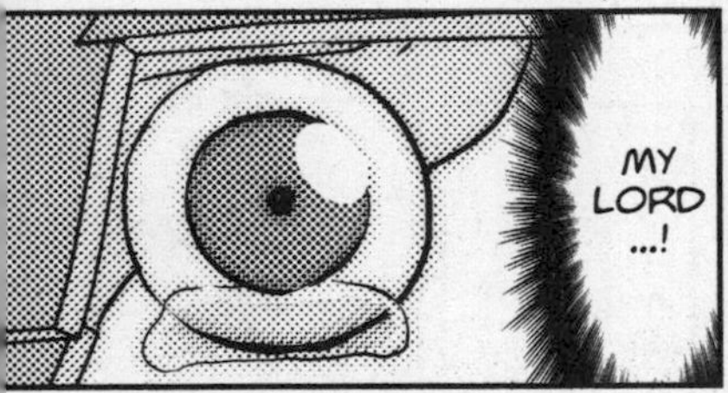
MY LORD ...!

THE FLOW OF TIME IS A TRAGIC THING, SHOGUNYAN...
I JOURNEYED TO JAPAN, I LEARNED THE WAY OF THE SAMURAI AND WE TRAINED TOGETHER. THOSE WERE THE DAYS...

THEN LET'S WORK TOGETHER AGAIN, LAST NYANMURAI!
...
A SAMURAI MAY NOT HAVE MULTIPLE LORDS. I ONLY HAVE ONE AND IT IS HE THAT NAMED ME.

HOWEVER...

...I CAN HELP YOU AS A FRIEND.

FSH...

HURRAY! ♪

POOPT

I GOT ANOTHER YO-KAI MEDAL! ♪

ALLOW ME TO INTRODUCE YOU TO SHOGUNYAN'S DESCENDANT...

...JIBANYAN!

THIS IS THE LAST NYANMURAI.

WHAAAAAAAT?!

HUUUUUH

NOT ANOTHER NYAN YO-KAI...!

THERE'S SO MANY OF THEM...

OH COME ON...

AND THIS IS TOMNYAN!

NICE TO MEET YOU! ♪

NATE ADAMS'S CURRENT NUMBER OF YO-KAI FRIENDS: 68

CHAPTER 107:
KNOCK SOME SENSE INTO THAT SLACKER!
FEATURING LAZY YO-KAI HORIZONTAIL
YOU CAN'T DECEIVE ME!
WHO ARE YOU REALLY?!

I'M NATE ADAMS, AN ORDINARY ELEMENTARY SCHOOL STUDENT.
WHAT IS HE TALKING ABOUT?!
EVER SINCE I GOT A YO-KAI WATCH, I'VE BEEN ABLE TO SEE YO-KAI.
I HAVE BEEN MEETING MORE YO-KAI FROM BBQ LATELY...
BMP BMP

A CRYPTIC CAT YO-KAI WHO LOOKS A LOT LIKE JIBANYAN...

TOM-NYAN.

AND A YO-KAI WHO HAS BEEN ALIVE SINCE TRAVELING TO JAPAN DURING THE WARRING STATES PERIOD...
LAST NYAN-MURAI.

YOUR ACCENT... I CAN TELL THERE'S SOME-THING OFF ABOUT IT!
AND THIS IS TOM-NYAN... HE'S FROM BBQ!
NICE TO MEET YOU! ♪
YOU'RE NOT FROM BBQ! I CAN TELL!
WHO ARE YOU AND WHERE DID YOU COME FROM ?!

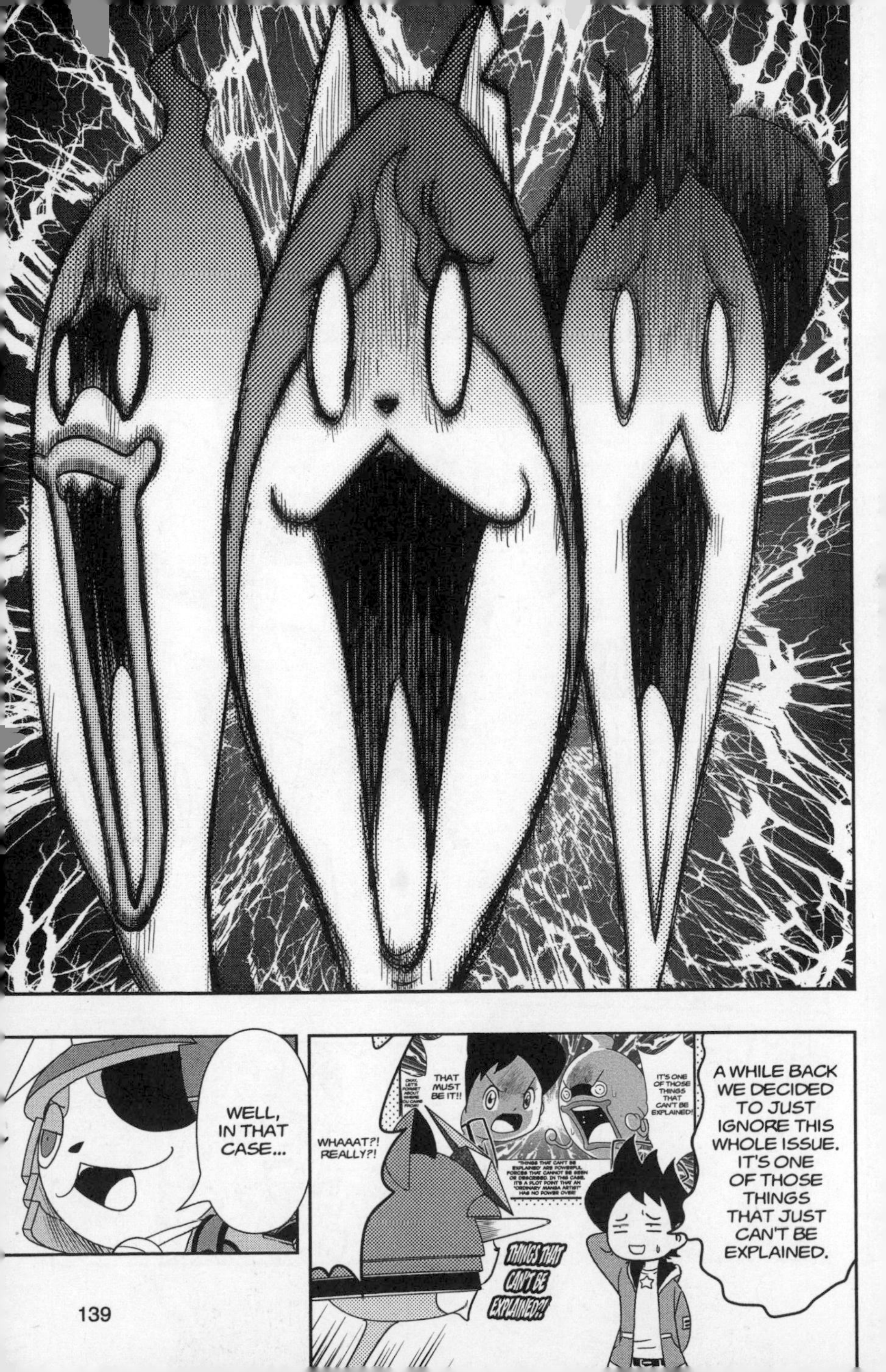

WELL, IN THAT CASE...

WHAAAT?! REALLY?!
OKAY, LET'S FORGET ABOUT WHERE YOU CAME FROM!
THAT MUST BE IT!!
IT'S ONE OF THOSE THINGS THAT CAN'T BE EXPLAINED!
A WHILE BACK WE DECIDED TO JUST IGNORE THIS WHOLE ISSUE. IT'S ONE OF THOSE THINGS THAT JUST CAN'T BE EXPLAINED.
"THINGS THAT CAN'T BE EXPLAINED" ARE POWERFUL FORCES THAT CANNOT BE SEEN OR DESCRIBED. IN THIS CASE, IT'S A PLOT POINT THAT AN "ORDINARY MANGA ARTIST" HAS NO POWER OVER!
THINGS THAT CAN'T BE EXPLAINED?!

I'LL ASK FOR FOR-GIVENESS.

PLEASE FORGIVE ME.

WAIT, WAIT, WAIT!

FUSSSH

WOW!

MY PLAN REQUIRES STRONG YO-KAI LIKE HIM.
EXCELLENT.
SAMURAI ALWAYS KEEP THEIR WORD, DON'T THEY? ♪
LAST NYANMURAI VALUES BUSHIDO, THE WAY OF THE SAMURAI.
THE WAY OF THE SAMURAI...
HMM...
GIVE ME A BREAK!
UGGGGH...
LIKE... WHAT'S THE POINT OF THIS ANYWAY?!
WHAT?! WHAT'S WRONG ?!
...

PEOPLE WILL COMPLAIN IF THIS STORY IS TOO VIOLENT!
WHAT ERA ARE YOU FROM? THIS IS SO OLD-SCHOOL AND INAPPROPRIATE.
OLD ...?
HEY!
SLASH

YOU WERE ASKING FOR IT, WHISPER.

ARE YOU ALL RIGHT?!

I CANNOT FORGIVE ANYONE WHO MOCKS THE WAY OF THE SAMURAI.

SWSH SWSH

A SAMURAI WON'T ATTACK AN UNARMED OPPONENT...

...BUT HIS DISHONORABLE WORDS COULDN'T GO UNPUNISHED!

CHIKT

TWITCH TWITCH

...

HUMPH...I WASN'T EXPECTING THAT!

WHAT?

PHEW! YOU'RE OKAY!

OWW.. HOW... COULD YOU...?

...
WHAT'S GOING ON?! IS THIS LAST NYANMURAI'S ABILITY?!
AIIIEEE-E-EE!
WHAT?! ANOTHER ME?!

ARRRRRGH!
NO! I'VE BEEN SLICED IN HALF!
I CAN'T EAT ANYTHING NOW BECAUSE IT'LL JUST FALL OUT!
THAT'S WHAT YOU'RE UPSET ABOUT?!
DASH
LAST NYAN-MURAI!
JIBANYAN'S MAD ABOUT WHAT HE DID TO WHISPER!
HOW COULD YOU DO THAT TO HIM?!
WUMPT
URGH ...
WUMPT
!!!
!!!

THAT'S NOT OKAY!
SPLU
NGKT
HUURRGNNH!
HEY...!!
HEY, WHISPER! JIBANYAN DIDN'T DO IT ON PURPOSE!
SORRY...
JUST... FORGET... ABOUT IT... WHAT A DRAG...
THIS IS SO STRANGE! WHISPER IS USUALLY PESKY AND OBNOXIOUS BUT HE GAVE UP SO FAST!
MAYBE THERE'S A QUICK-SURRENDER YO-KAI INSPIRITING HIM?!
FWAAASH
HEY, NATE...

PFFFFFT
A QUICK-SURRENDER YO-KAI?! WHAT KIND OF LAME IDEA IS THAT?!
HA HA HA HA
EVEN CHOPPED IN HALF, HE'S STILL OBNOX-IOUS.

NZOOOO...
I'VE BEEN INSPIRITED BY A YO-KAI THAT MAKES EVERYTHING FEEL LIKE A DRAG.
UGH...EVEN EXPLAINING IT IS A DRAG...
SO YOU ARE BEING INSPIRITED AFTER ALL!
And the Yo-kai looks really weird!

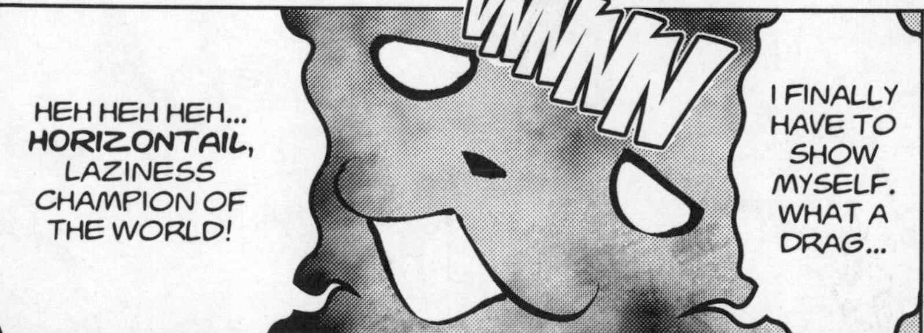
VNNNNN
I FINALLY HAVE TO SHOW MYSELF. WHAT A DRAG...
HEH HEH HEH... HORIZONTAIL, LAZINESS CHAMPION OF THE WORLD!

UGGGGH
COWER IN MY PRESENCE! HOWL AND WAIL IN FEAR!
THAT'S WHAT THEY CALL ME!
...
LAZY YO-KAI HORIZONTAIL
WHAT'S THIS GUY'S DEAL? CAN'T HE AT LEAST STAND UP?
WHAT A DRAG! WHY SHOULD I?!
SEEMS LIKE A PRETTY USE-LESS YO-KAI...
NO! DON'T UNDERESTI-MATE HIM!
BOOOOM
I'VE BEEN INSPIRITED BY HIM, SO I KNOW...HE HAS ANOTHER HIDDEN ABILITY!
?!
AS PROOF... I'M... HAVING... URGH...

HUFF HUFF

I'M HAVING TROUBLE BREATH-ING AND...I'M STARTING... TO LOSE... CONSCIOUS-NESS...

THAT'S NOT BECAUSE OF HIM! YOU WERE CUT IN HALF!

TWITCH TWITCH TWITCH TWITCH

WHAT
?
HUNH
INSTEAD, WHY DON'T YOU ALL JUST GROVEL ON THE GROUND BEFORE ME AND SAY, "YOU WIN."
Then you can leave.

YOU CAN'T MAKE US DO THAT! THIS FOREST BELONGS TO EVERYONE!
TAKE CARE OF HIM, JIBAN-YAN!
WHAAAAA
HE'S LAZY TOO! HE'S ALREADY BEEN INSPIRITED!
NOPE
...

DON'T WORRY! I WON'T USE MY SWORD AGAINST AN UNARMED OPPONENT!

!!!

VOOOSH

AN UNMOTIVATED YO-KAI! HOW SHAMEFUL! I'LL KNOCK SOME SENSE INTO YOU!

HE SAID HE WAS GOING TO TAKE A NAP SINCE THERE WERE ALREADY SO MANY OTHER CHARACTERS IN THIS CHAPTER.

ZZZooo ZZZooo

HMM HMM

OH, BROTHER
...

HI-YAAAH! *Pull yourself together!*

...

KRAKT

MEEOOOOOOW!

HE'S TRYING TO MOTIVATE JIBANYAN?!

WHOOPS...I KNOCKED HIM UNCONSCIOUS...

HE'S NOT JUST UNCONSCIOUS...I SEE SOMETHING COMING OUT OF HIM!

I'LL TAKE CARE OF THIS. PHYSICAL FIGHTING IS POINTLESS AGAINST A YO-KAI LIKE HIM.

TOMNYAN, YOU'VE GOT A PLAN?!

YOU'RE FASCINATING! TELL ME MORE ABOUT YOURSELF! ♪
I'LL PRETEND TO SYMPATHIZE WITH HIM TO GET HIM ON OUR SIDE!
I SEE! TOMNYAN'S TRYING TO WARM UP TO HIM!
...
YES! YO-KAI LIKE HIM OPEN UP EASILY IF YOU'RE KIND TO THEM!
YOU WANT TO KNOW... ABOUT ME?!
!!!
I'D RATHER NOT! MYSELF... SEEMS LIKE A DRAG.
YOU SEEM LIKE A SMART GUY. WHY DON'T YOU GO TAKE CARE OF THEM FOR ME?
NO! HE'S TAKING MY KINDNESS FOR GRANTED! HE'S TREATING ME LIKE HIS SERVANT!

HOW DARE YOU! CENTI-CUFFS!!
CHOOM
CHOOM
CHOOM
I THOUGHT YOU SAID WE SHOULDN'T FIGHT!
DRA-A-AAA
?!
MEOW, MEOW, MEOOOOW...
FSSH FSSH FSSH
ANYONE WHO GETS CLOSE TO ME LOSES ALL THEIR MOTIVATION!
AH HA
SOME YO-KAI EXIST ONLY TO DO PEOPLE HARM...
BUT THERE ARE OTHERS, LIKE ME, WHO CHOOSE TO HELP PEOPLE!
YOU'RE FORTUNATE TO WALK UPON THIS WORLD... DON'T YOU WANT TO LEAD A FULFILLING LIFE?
KRCH
NAW... SOUNDS LIKE A DRAG.

VOOOOSH
THAT'S ENOUGH! I SHALL DO AWAY WITH YOU AND YOUR DESPICABLE ATTITUDE!
NO! DON'T GET NEAR HIM!
THE LAZINESS ISN'T AFFECTING LAST NYANMURAI!
WOOOSH
WHAAAT?! MY POWERS... THEY'RE NOT WORKING ON YOU!

SHUP
HA! NOW THEY'RE WORKING! FIGHTING SEEMS LIKE SUCH A DRAG, DOESN'T IT?!
HEH HEH
I... I...
...AS A SAMURAI...I CANNOT ATTACK AN UNARMED OPPONENT.
EVEN WHEN THREATENED WITH DEFEAT... HE STILL FOLLOWS THE WAY OF THE SAMURAI!
HE TRULY IS THE LAST SAMURAI YO-KAI!
NOW, WHILE HIS GUARD'S DOWN, I'LL HIT HIM WITH MY POWERS ONCE AGAIN!
I...I...

...I DON'T CARE ANYMORE. WHAT A DRAG.
SLASH
ARRRRGH!
HE WAS SO DISIN-TERESTED THAT HE BROKE THE SAMURAI'S CREED!
I'VE BEEN... DEFEATED... BY SOMEONE WHO GREW...
...TOO LAZY...
I'M SORRY. FROM NOW ON...

...I'LL GOING TO BE ALL FIRED UP!
WHAAAAA
YOU'RE NOT ACTING LIKE SOMEONE WHO'S LEARNED THEIR LESSON!
HEY, COME ON...IT'S OKAY.

IF YOU PUSH YOURSELF TOO HARD YOU'LL WEAR OUT QUICKLY. AND WHEN PEOPLE DISAGREE WITH YOU, YOU LASH OUT INSTEAD OF LEARNING ABOUT WHAT YOU DID WRONG.
...

HMM... YOU KNOW YOUR STUFF.
YOU'RE THE FIRST PERSON WHO HASN'T TRIED TO LECTURE ME!

ALTHOUGH IT'S STILL KIND OF A DRAG.
LECTURES ARE A DRAG, BUT IF YOU AREN'T GIVING ME ONE...I GUESS WE CAN BE FRIENDS.
FSH...
OOH. ♪

PO
PT
I GOT ANOTHER YO-KAI MEDAL. ♪

...

I SEE.

THAT'S HOW HE KEEPS GAINING FRIENDS.

NATE ADAMS IS SUCH A STRANGE FELLOW.
HE CERTAINLY IS...HE REMINDS ME A BIT OF "YOU-KNOW-WHO."

YES... OUR LORD...I SEE IT TOO.

HEY, SO YOU BOTH SERVED THE SAME LORD?
YES, HE WAS A MAN WHO HAD NO FEAR OF YO-KAI.
AND HE COULD SEE YOU, EVEN WITHOUT A YO-KAI WATCH?
THAT'S RIGHT.

WOW... AMAZING.

FOR TWO LEGENDARY YO-KAI TO OPEN UP TO HIM, HE MUST HAVE BEEN A TRULY GREAT MAN.

WHISPER TAUGHT ME THAT YO-KAI CAN ONLY BE SEEN BY HUMANS THEY TRULY TRUST.

...
THE ONLY YO-KAI I'M THAT CLOSE TO IS WHISPER.
I HOPE TO BE LIKE HIM ONE DAY!
...

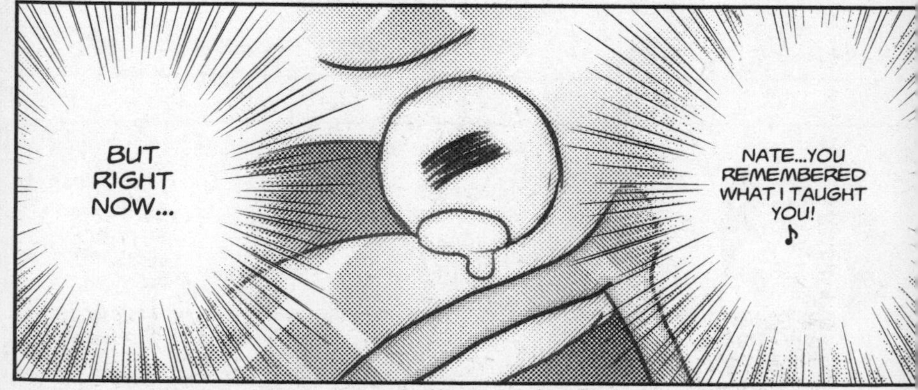

BUT RIGHT NOW...
NATE...YOU REMEMBERED WHAT I TAUGHT YOU! ♪

I'M GOING TO DO IT!
...YOU DON'T ACTUALLY SEE ME, DO YOU?!
THUNCK
NATE ADAMS'S CURRENT NUMBER OF YO-KAI FRIENDS: 69

CHAPTER 108:
ERASE YOUR FLAWS BY BEING REBORN!
FEATURING REBORN YO-KAI SKILLSKULL

HIS NAME IS TOMNYAN.

AND A SINGLE THOUGHT DOMINATES HIS MIND.

HE FIRST APPEARED...
...AS A CRYPTIC YO-KAI.

BUT HE HASN'T APPEARED...
...IN MANY SCENES SINCE.

TOMNYAN!
GET OUTTA HERE! I'M DOING MY BIG, DRAMATIC INTRODUCTION!

BUT A TRUCK'S COMING...

ARRRGGGH!

VRROOM

CRYPTIC YO-KAI TOMNYAN

IT'S ALREADY BEEN SEVERAL MONTHS SINCE I CAME HERE...

WHY DIDN'T YOU... SAY THAT... FIRST...?

YOU SHOULDN'T DAYDREAM WHILE TRAINING IN THE STREET.

BY USING NATE ADAMS AND ALL THE YO-KAI HE KNOWS...
ARE YOU OKAY?
...I'LL FINALLY BE ABLE TO FULFILL MY PURPOSE! THE ENTIRE REASON I CAME HERE!

BUT I, TOMNYAN...
...I MUST BECOME STRONGER...

...IF I WISH TO FULFILL MY DESTINY!

NATE'S RIGHT! STOP DAY-DREAMING! YOU NEED TO PAY ATTEN-TION!!

SORRY.

HUH?

VRROOM
ARRRRGH!
YOU NEED TO PAY ATTENTION TOO.
JIBANYAN

HA HA HA! DON'T WORRY, NATE! AS LONG AS I'M HERE, YOU'VE GOT NO PROBLEM!
NO MATTER WHAT THOSE GOOFBALLS DO, I'LL BE THE STRAIGHT MAN IN THIS COMIC!
BAAM
ARE YOU OKAY?
TWITCH TWITCH...
GREAT... NOW WE HAVE TWO GAG CHARACTERS!
THIS IS GETTING RIDICULOUS...
ORDINARY ELEMENTARY SCHOOL STUDENT NATE ADAMS

THUNK!
WE'LL KEEP EVERYTHING MOVING—
THEY'RE ALL GOOF-BALLS!
ÜURRGH!
VRROOOM
NATE'S BUTLER WHISPER
I FORGOT THERE WERE THREE GAG CHARACTERS...
YOU SHOULD PAY MORE ATTENTION!
I KNOW! MAYBE
DAIZ IS AROUND ?!
MAYBE!
FWAASH
ZSSSH
?!
USELESS, DULL, MEDIOCRE ...
DISTASTEFUL, TROUBLE-SOME, EASILY DISTRACTED...
BUT I'LL GIVE THEM ALL ANOTHER CHANCE! ♪

I AM SKILLSKULL! I'VE COME TO REMAKE YOU! I'VE COME TO RATTLE YOUR BONES!
...
DELAYED REACTION! NO POINTS!
YOU'RE GONNA GET RE-BORN!
THE FISH PLACE

WHAP
BAM BOOM!
KRASH
MEOW!
JIBANYAN!
ANYONE STRUCK BY MY HAM-MER...
...IS REBORN WITH THEIR FLAWS CORRECT-ED!
THAT'S
...
THAT'S ...
SHUFF
...SKILL-SKULL, A YO-KAI THAT TRANSFORMS GOOD-FOR-NOTHING PEOPLE INTO PRODUCTIVE ONES!
WHAT? HE'S A GOOD YO-KAI?
...
OKAY, JIBANYAN! SHOW THEM WHAT YOU'VE BECOME!
IT'S PROBA-BLY JUST A FUNNY FACE OR SOME WEIRD JOKE...
Nothing off-color, please...

WHAAAAT?!
I HIT HIM TOO HARD!
HEY...

UNGK
HEY!
SHOOM
YOU KNOCKED HIM BACK INTO HIS BODY?!
MMNGH...
WOW! HE'S COMING BACK AROUND!
PHEW! ARE YOU OKAY?

GOOD AFTER-NOON. ♪

THANK YOU SO MUCH FOR YOUR CONCERN. ♪

...
HE'S POLITE! AND SO FORMAL!
DOES THIS MEAN... HE'S BEEN REBORN?!

BUT I THOUGHT HE WAS RE-CREATED TO REACT QUICKER..

MAY I ASK YOU A QUES-TION?
UM... SURE?

BOOOOOONE
WHERE AM I? AND WHO AM I?
HE GOT HIT SO HARD HE LOST HIS MEMORY!
THAT EXPLAINS IT...
FSSH
TA-DAAH!
UMMMM...
DON'T "TA-DAAH" ME! YOU FAILED!
YOU'RE RIGHT ...
BUT DON'T WORRY. I FAIL ALL THE TIME!
DUUUUUH
I CAN TELL!
JIBANYAN, ARE YOU—
OH.

KA-THUNGKT

HNNGH

TWITCH

TWITCH

ARE YOU OKAY?

MEOW?
NATE, WHISPER... MY BODY HURTS... ALL OVER...
OOH!
GETTING HIT RESTORED HIS MEMORY!

TA-DAAH!
!?!
HEY! YOU DIDN'T DO THAT!
FSH

AH...!

HEEEEY!
VSSH
?
I WAS HIT!
THEN TOOK A HAMMER TO THE HEAD!
I LOST MY MEMORY!
AND THEN GOT HIT AGAIN!
WHAT KIND OF A JOKE IS THIS?!
...
CLOMPT CLOMPT
YEEAAH!
CLOMPT CLOMPT
PERFECT REACTION! 100 POINTS!
AMAZING!
WHAT DOES HE GET POINTS FOR?!
HE'S JUST SHOUTING!
THIS IS WHAT IT MEANS TO BE REBORN!
THIS IS NUTS...
JIBANYAN, YOU'RE GETTING HIT BY TOO MANY TRUCKS.
MEOW...
SIGH...I DON'T WANT TO GET HIT ANYMORE...
SOMEONE WHO NEVER GETS HIT BY TRUCKS! BE...
WHAP BAM BOOM!

WH...
WHAT?!
I FEEL IT... AN INCREDIBLE POWER...!
RRRRR
BMBL
HIS POWER... IT'S... AMAZING...!
HE'S BEEN REBORN ONCE AGAIN!
EVEN IF I FACE ANOTHER TRUCK, I WON'T GET HIT AGAIN! I KNOW IT!
GRRRRRR

HE GOT RUN OVER.

KRA-DOOOM

VROOOOM

I'M COUNTING ON YOU!
A BODY THAT WON'T GET HIT, WON'T GET RUN OVER AND CAN DEFEAT A TRUCK! WHAP BAM BOOM!
THUNGK
IF I CAN'T BEAT THE TRUCK, WHAT GOOD IS BEING REBORN?!
THIS IS RIDICULOUS! IT'S NOT FAIR!
IT DIDN'T HIT ME, BUT IT STILL RAN ME OVER!
PERFECT REACTION. 100 POINTS.

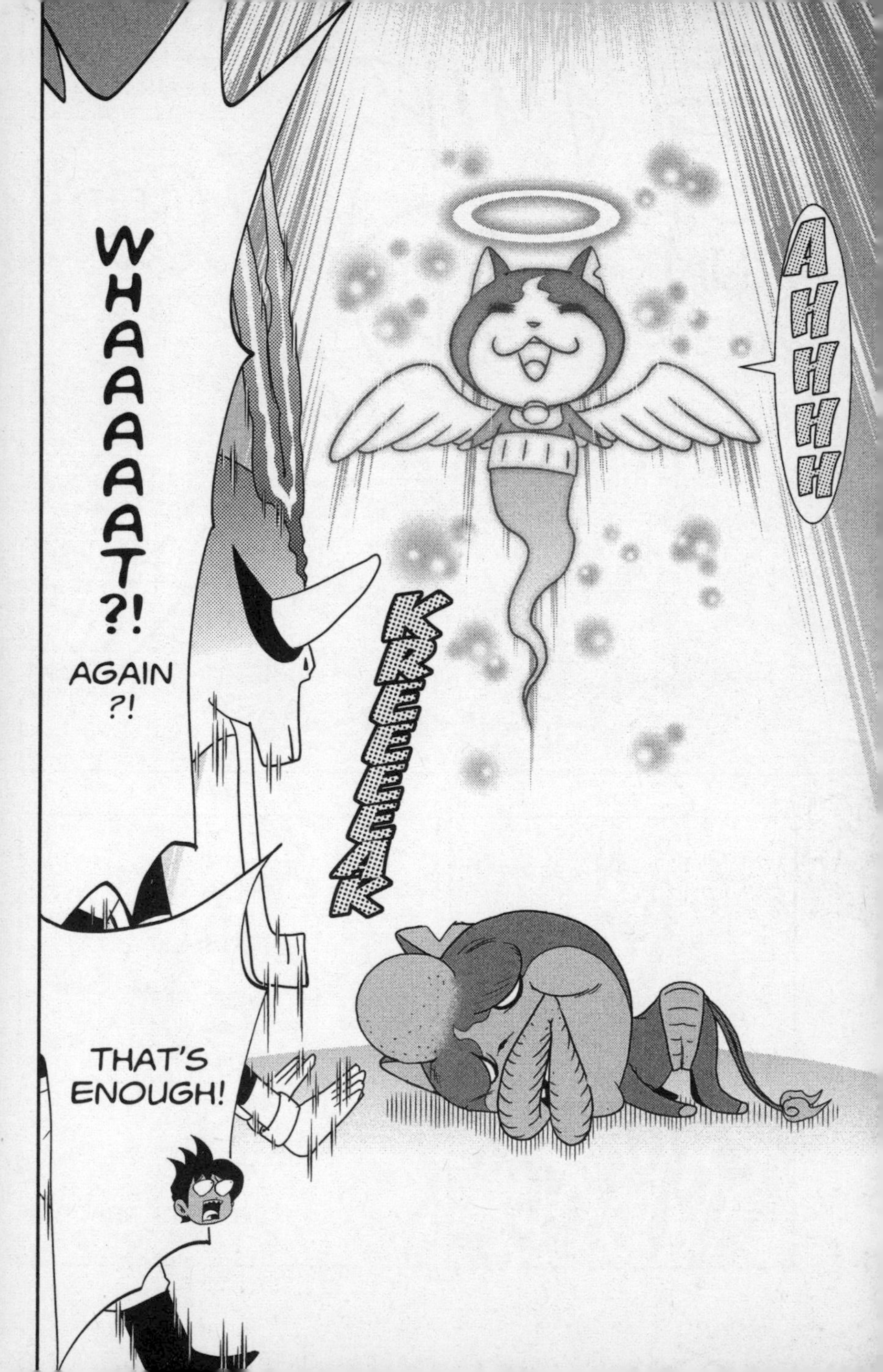
AHHHH
KREEEEAK
WHAAAAAT?!
AGAIN ?!
THAT'S ENOUGH!

CLUMPT
BOOSH
GET BACK IN THERE!
SHUPT
YOU'RE SO VIOLENT!
He just threw him back in!
HAH!
MMNGH...
LOOK OUT! A TRUCK!
PAWS OF—
VRROOM
HE'S PROBABLY GOING TO LOSE IN A DIFFERENT WAY...

FUUUURY!!
CHOO
CHOOM
CHOOM
CHOOM
CHOOM
CHOOM
WHAT?!
WHAT?!

WHAAAAAAT?!
HE... PUNCHED THE TRUCK AWAY...!
I...
I DID IT!
ARRRRRGH!
KRUNCHT
HE GOT CRUSHED.
INCREDIBLE...
I DIDN'T GET HIT! OR RUN OVER! I'M NOT AFRAID OF TRUCKS ANYMORE!
HE LOST AFTER ALL.
I'LL MAKE SURE THE TRUCK AND DRIVER ARE REBORN.

HEH HEH HEH, I CAME HERE BECAUSE I WANTED TO HELP PEOPLE MORE.
THOUGH THE RESULTS AREN'T ALWAYS GREAT... YOU HAVE AN AMAZING ABILITY!
CALL ME WHENEVER YOU OR SOMEONE ELSE NEEDS TO BE REBORN.
FSH
WOW! THANKS A LOT. ♪
POPT
I GOT ANOTHER YO-KAI MEDAL. ♪
IT'S A RARE OCCASION WHEN YOU CAN BECOME FRIENDS WITH A YO-KAI WITHOUT FIGHTING THEM! ♪
I'M GONNA RE-CREATE ALL SORTS OF THINGS!
I WANT TO BE REBORN TOO! ♪ I'M TIRED OF BEING JUST "ORDINARY!"
LEAVE IT TO ME !!
WOOOOOSH
BUT IF HE FAILS... YOU'LL DIE!
!!

SWOOSH
HE'S RIGHT! I WON'T DO IT!
I'LL CHANGE MYSELF THROUGH HARD WORK AND TURNING OVER A NEW LEAF!
ヒョイ

HEEEY!
ZWOO
WOOOAH!

SHUNCK!
URRRNGGH!
SORRY!

OWW...MAYBE... MAYBE HITTING MYSELF... HAS FIXED MY FLAWS...? MAYBE I WON'T...FAIL ANYMORE? ♪
MAYBE. ♪
OH?

REST IN PEACE.
YEEAAH!
BEING REBORN ROCKS!

NATE ADAMS'S CURRENT NUMBER OF YO-KAI FRIENDS: 70

WHERE AM I? WHO AM I...?
TWITCH TWITCH
...
I WAS BARELY EVEN IN THIS CHAPTER...

CHAPTER 109: BLAST AWAY THE COLD! ①

VRROOM
SKRUNCH
HEEEY!
WHAT?!

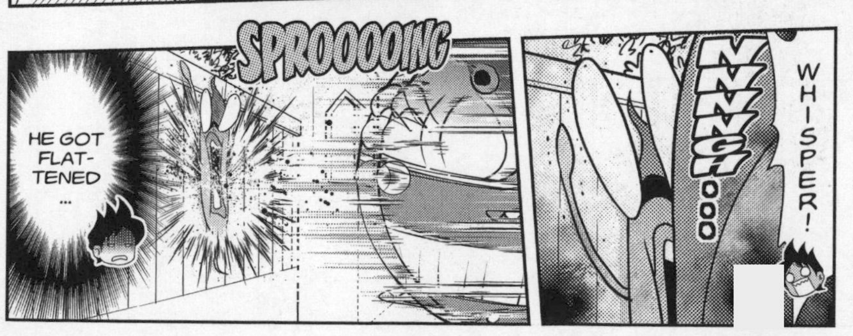

HEY...

KRA-THOOM

ARRRRRGH!

WHISPER, ARE YOU OKAY?!
BOING BOING
WOW! THAT WAS A SURPRISE!
I DIDN'T EVEN GET HURT THANKS TO MY BOUNCY, ROUND BODY! BEING ROUND IS GREAT! ♪
BOING BOING
NOW'S NOT THE TIME, JIBANYAN!

HUUUURNG

HIS FACE SWELLED UP! HE'S COMPLETELY ROUND!

WOW! NOW YOU CAN BOUNCE AROUND TOO! ♪

BLAST AWAY THE COLD!! ②

AHHH, THAT'S BETTER!

DON'T USE MY TAIL LIKE A BONFIRE!

FSSSH FSSSH

So that's what you wanted!

I DON'T WANT YOU TO COOK ME!
PFFFFT
WHAT ARE YOU EVEN TALKING ABOUT?!
TWITCH TWITCH
IT'D BE SO EASY...TO PULL THE TRIGGER...

OH! A PISTOL!
IT'S NOT A GUN! IT'S LASER BLASTER!
REALLY? SHOW ME HOW IT WORKS!
KRRKT
YOU'VE SEEN ME USE IT BEFORE... WATCH CARE-FULLY THIS TIME!

SEE?
ZZAAPT
AHHH... IT'S SO WARM! ♪
Ha ha ha. ♪
...
SO THAT'S WHAT YOU WANTED.
IF YOU REALLY WANT TO WARM UP THAT BADLY...

WHOA! WHOA!

ZZZAPT

ZZZAPT

...THIS SHOULD DO THE TRICK!!!